Privy to the Mayors Council / The Helper
(A Two Story Anthology)

Also published by New Guild

Melody for Lizzy
S.O.S Men against the Sea
Elvis in Wonderland

Privy to the Mayor's Council

The Helper

A Two Story Anthology

Paul Lehman

A New Guild Book

Published by New Era Writer's Guild (UK) Ltd
5 Cogdean Walk, Corfe Mullen
Wimborne Minster, Dorset BH21 3XB

PO Box 11476
Bloubergrant 7443, South Africa
Tel: (+21) 557 6281
Fax (+21) 557 0704

PO Box 100 806
North Shore Mail Centre
Auckland 10, New Zealand
Tel/Fax: (+9) 443 8069

ISBN 1 899694 15 3

This book was designed by
Crispin Goodall Design Ltd
463 Ashley Road
Poole, Dorset BH14 OAX

Printed in the Republic of South Africa by
CTP Book Printers (Pty) Ltd
P.O. Box 6060 Parow East 7501

CONTENTS

Privy to the Mayor's Council

Paul Lehman

PREFACE

Palmpoppiesfontein is an imaginary town in the Orange Free State. It has a range of mountains and a river. It also has an intriguing diversity of inhabitants. The district is farmed by Great Trek descendants. The town itself has attracted those who would grow fat on the commercial fruits of the surrounding farmers' labour. When oil is discovered on a nearby farm, avarice, greed and lust for power surface with a vengeance.

None of these characters exists. If by any chance you recognise the place or identify yourself or your friends with any of these people of my mind, then I can but offer you my deepest sympathy and condolatory bunches of khaki weed.

Chapter 1

'Of course we'll have to change the name of the town,' said the Mayor confidently. He was shaken by the immediate negative response of his councillors who jumped to their feet and protested volubly.

'But gentlemen,' he said severely, 'you can't be serious. How can we possibly continue with the name Palmpoppiesfontein when, in a few years' time we will be a metropolis bigger than Johannesburg?'

'An' wot is wrong with Palmpoppiesfontein?' asked fat councillor van der Watt, thrusting out his jaw aggressively.

'Are you trying to destroy our heritage?' yipped little Lappies LeRoux, with a nervous flutter of his hands and overwhelmed by his own audacity.

Most gratifyingly to LeRoux, a fresh uproar broke out in support of their heritage. Van der Watt's jaw seemed dislocated, it protruded so alarmingly. The Mayor banged on the table.

'Gentlemen, we must be reasonable. This is a case in which 'a rose by any other name would not smell as sweet.'

'Now he says we schtink!' shouted Heinz Gruber, whose mental processes were rather limited. Nobody had ever quite understood how he had been elected to the town council; he hadn't even the sense to offer bribes.

'No, no, I'm not suggesting anything at all like that,' protested the Mayor, 'but a name has a great deal of importance. As a little farming community, Palmpoppiesfontein is adequately named. In fact it sounds perfect, you know, restful. But it would be very wrong to apply such a name to an industrial and mining giant such as our town will soon become. Come, gentlemen, what is more important? Tradition and heritage or ... money?'

He had played an ace of trumps. As a group of men supposedly working for the good of their town, their avarice was matched only by their hypocrisy and outweighed their other attributes, good or bad. They had carefully prevented any conflicting business or professional men from acquiring licences to open shops or businesses or to set up practice in town.

Palmpoppiesfontein had its two lawyers, whose interest in the law was minimal, its two accountants who could miscount when advantageous and its two doctors who were at the time rounding off a very successful campaign on appendectomies to pay for their new BMWs.

The Mayor had the only pharmacy in the town and other chemists had long ago given up applying for licences to flog pills in Palmpoppiesfontein. The Mayor argued that the town could never support two pharmacies, so it would be impractical to permit another and cause them both to starve. He ignored the fact that Bisley's Pharmacy netted him about ninety thousand rand per annum plus an occasional overseas holiday.

Councillor van der Watt was the local grocer and had owned the town's only provision store of any significance for many years. He intended to keep it that way, maintaining that the mark up on foodstuffs was such that his living was precarious.

His Mercedes Benz, he said, was bought with money inherited by his wife. Councillor Morison, one of the two lawyers, had been the correspondent of the Bloemfontein attorneys who had handled Mrs van der Watt's inheritance and he knew that it had been R157,33. The temptation to violate what was left of his professional code had been almost irresistible and one day he knew he would have to 'drop' the grocer.

Morison, although proclaiming loudly that there was enough for all, chose to ignore the fact that all votes for applying attorneys were declined 100% against.

Councillor Heinz Gruber, whose father had been an immigrant motor engineer from Düsseldorf, was the proud owner of the town's only garage.

Bisley's reference to money had them worried. If the town's name was an obstacle to their bank balances, then it would have to go, and to hell with tradition.

Attorney Morison said, 'Mr Mayor, if we did decide to change the name of the town, just what would we call it?'

Bisley squirmed with pleasure. Good old Rory was right on cue. He was a very influential member of the council and a respected citizen who had been mayor himself for a few years before Bisley, who had now held office for nearly eight years.

During seven and seven eighths of those years the town had not progressed at all, but now the Big Discovery had blasted everyone out of any complacency. The ordinary citizens were eagerly awaiting the boom and a large proportion of them were happily sitting on the fence to watch the vested interests going to blazes.

Mayor Bisley had given birth to the idea of a change of name for the town and fondly conjured up images of 'Bisley' or 'Bisleyburg'. He had even made tentative enquiries at Province concerning a change of motor registration from the current ungainly OPP to, possibly, OBY. Of course he was far too modest to voice his choice of name outright.

'Well,' he replied gazing at the ceiling meditatively, 'it should be a name in recognition of someone connected with the town and its present events. As a start, for discussion, I would suggest we consider the name of the man through whom all this is possible, whose discovery has placed us on the threshold of a boom such as this country has never seen before.'

Bisley was not embarrassed by the fact that the man referred to rejoiced in the name of Sarel Labuschagne, clearly unusable in town naming, and that he was currently lying face downwards on his bed of pain in Bloemfontein hospital, while doctors removed splinters of timber and sundry foreign bodies from his withered buttocks.

'Ag, man,' snorted van der Watt, 'how can you call a town anything like 'Labuschagne'? No *mense,* I reckon Palmpoppiesfontein was good enough for Potgieter, de Wet and all our forefathers and it must be good enough for us. It would *darem* be an insult to try to change it. Even for money.'

This last remark drew startled glances from the rest of the council. They were perhaps not as far-sighted as van der Watt. He realised that in his line of business he would be the first to feel the paradoxical pinch of expansion. The professional men would not be overwhelmed too easily by squatters coming into a boom town; there were certain ethics connected with the professions.

But when people in their thousands streamed into town, booming as Palmpoppiesfontein would, the first requirement was going to be food. In no time the supermarkets would flash their gaudy signs, enticing canned music and cutthroat prices. Van der Watt would be the first to bite the dust.

For all his ineffectualness, Lappies LeRoux was no birdbrain and he realised at once that van der Watt had twigged something that so far had eluded the others. Lappies had a clothing shop, whence his nickname which he fervently preferred to the tragedy of his baptism which had saddled him with Bonatius Albertus.

Although he felt that van der Watt had some good reason for his opposition to the Mayor's suggestion, Lappies was intrigued by the idea of a new name for the town. His family had been in the area since the Great Trek and his was certainly the oldest name. He had no reason to believe that it had been one of his ancestors who had originally named the place. He must have been an imaginative man for neither palms and poppies nor springs of water were in evidence anywhere.

In any event, Lappies cherished the image of honour and the vicarious glory of anything to which he could attach himself. He had sweated like a bull to reach the town council and broke the tenth commandment every time he looked at Bisley's chain of office. A change of name to LeRouxville or Rouxburg would lead inevitably to his own election as mayor.

Morison snorted in van der Watt's direction. 'Mr van der Watt is to be admired, gentlemen,' he smirked. 'I wish I had his loyalty to tradition. I am forcibly attracted to anything which spells gain for me. However, I feel that this is an instance where our own feelings and also our own pockets are secondary. The future prosperity of this town rests with our common sense and clear thinking. And you must surely realise that no one should suffer as the result of a boom.'

It gave him great pleasure to voice the private thoughts of them all as he said: 'After all, we still control the influx of business. We will be in on the ground floor of the boom and the rest will have to await our pleasure.'

Bisley's emotions were mixed. His admiration of Morison's eloquence and his appreciation of his friend's defence of the Mayoral proposition were limited by his annoyance of Morison's take over of the meeting and his upstaging of Bisley's own well-practised speech. He rapped on the table.

'Gentlemen, I wish to thank councillor Morison for his clear appreciation of the position. Now we must get down to facts. We must decide whether or not we are to change the name from Palmpoppiesfontein to Bis ... er ... to something more befitting our future character. I would vote for a change of name and I gather that councillor Morison would support me and councillor van der Watt would oppose. Now I would like an expression of each councillor's vote and reasons, please.'

There was silence. Lappies fiddled with his fingers and van der Watt worked his jaws. Morison smiled and leaned back in his chair, joining the tips of his fingers. Heinz Gruber had lost the drift and decided to wait for someone else to speak in the hope that the subject would become clearer. The other two members of the group were Felix Drumpel, the undertaker, and Angus McTiver, one of the town's two doctors.

Drumpel's long horselike face did not look happy – it was doubtful that the face ever wore such an expression. Naturally a lugubrious man, he was ponderously considering the problem. The Discovery had jolted him along with everyone else, now this emergency meeting of the council had taken him by surprise. The radical nature of the Mayor's suggestion had shoved him even further up the creek. However, the word money kept cropping up and a boom meant more people, more deaths, more business. He cared nothing for the name or its removal as long as he had enough time to change his stationery if necessary.

Angus McTiver struggled to focus his mind on the problem and his eyes on the Mayor. It was far too early in the morning for him to rise above the vapours of last night's whisky. The pub opened at ten and here he was at nine thirty being asked to consider what appeared to be matters of national importance.

It had been agreed for some time between Angus and his partner, Corny Bezuidenhout, that Angus was unavailable until midday. His consulting was done from two until five. If Corny was overloaded with operations and it became necessary for Angus to take some poor unfortunate's life in his quivering hands, it would be at five p.m. only. The rest of McTiver's time was spent in (a) drinking and (b) recovering from drinking.

Strangely enough he was a good doctor, the word being applicable to his technical proficiency if not his habits. It was he who had discovered the cash potential of the appendix and had talked young Corny into the scheme. As he said: 'Any gutsache can be deeagnosed as appendicitis – who can argue wi' us? At foor hunnert rands a time we'll clean up an' save a lot o' pipple trouble in later life. They'll enjooy a nice quiet operation noo instead of a rushed wun later in life.'

Corny agreed, but found himself treating the majority of their patients as most people preferred his steady hand and inoffensive breath to that of the scruffy little Scot whose ability, certainly most impressive, was becoming more and more adversely affected by alcohol.

Evidence of their campaign was freely available at the local swimming bath where, except on Sundays, scars of great imagination vied with each other on abdomens of every description.

'Come, gentlemen', said the Mayor. 'We have very little time in which to consider one of the greatest decisions we will ever have to make. Mr Drumpel, please, what would your opinion be?'

'The name means nothing to me,' the undertaker said slowly. 'I respect those who wish to retain the town's name for reasons of history or whatever and I also understand why some might feel that our funny name could be a bar to commercial progress, but personally I have no preference. I think that if this town is going to develop nothing will stop it, certainly not a name. Money is more powerful than good taste.'

'Thank you for the clear expression of your view, Mr Drumpel.' Bisley was displeased. Drumpel's remarks about the inexorable push of business had a ring of truth which could influence the other councillors to collectively consign 'Bisleyburg' to limbo. Bisley looked at Lappies who was staring fixedly at the Mayoral chain of office.

'Mr LeRoux?'

Lappies jumped. He had been in a delightful brown study, dreaming of a huge department store where hundreds of staff conducted business on his behalf while Mayor Lappies of Rouxburg drove in the Mayoral Rolls-Royce from function to function.

'Er ... er ... yes, Mr Mayor?' he spluttered.

'Your opinion please,' Bisley said contemptuously as if the question were only a matter of form. He was agreeably surprised when, with a nervous look at van der Watt, Lappies said, 'I agree that the name must be changed. A complete break with our present is necessary to create a new image for our town.'

He had surprised himself and grinned sickly at van der Watt who looked at him malevolently as his anger grew.

'Bolgat!' he swore at Lappies. 'What the hell do you know about images of towns, business, big business? All you can do is measure cloth and wrap up underpants.'

Lappies was annoyed by this cruelty. Feeling the support of the others, he did not cringe, but scowled back at the grocer and replied: 'And what have you learned about big business while slicing bacon and selling tins of beans?'

There was a ripple of laughter around the table as van der Watt threw his cigar angrily into the ash tray. He couldn't think of a suitable reply but growled and grumbled into his chest.

'Now, now, gentlemen,' said the Mayor oiling the troubled water. 'We must not let our judgement be clouded by personal matters. So far I gather that Mr van der Watt is the only one against the proposal. What of you, Dr McTiver?'

Angus squinted at his wristwatch and sighed with relief. 'Och, weel, Bisley, I furrst would like tae heer from Heinz, but if ye'll jest excuse me a wee minnit.' He rose and scurried out of the room and down the corridor to the Gents. Safely inside the WC, he dragged a nip flask from his hip pocket and tilted it to his lips, feeling the blessed relief course through him. It was not safe to consume his life-saver until the clock said it could be recharged.

He toddled back into the council chamber, jaunty of step and fooling none of the councillors by fiddling with his fly as he entered on a wave of White Horse.

'Noo,' he said briskly, rubbing his hands together, 'I hae ma oon idees aboot this matter, but let's furrst heer frum yew, Heinzie me lad.'

Gruber was still a bit bewildered by all the talk but he sensed that he should say something before they thought he was no use on the council. He took a deep breath.

'I agree, the name does stink ...' He was interrupted by the Mayor, who beamed at him and said: 'Definitely a swing in favour of a more suitable name. Thank you Mr Gruber. Now, Dr McTiver?'

'Theer's jest one wee thing which I think yew've all overluked.' He paused and looked at each of them in turn. When the anticipation began to quiver on their faces he said blandly,

'Yew've all forgotten that we'll have tae let in the bluidy Jews!'

There was a gasp followed by a shocked silence. Booms, town names, everything faded into insignificance. They were so busy contemplating their future prosperity that they had forgotten that where there was big business and big money, there were the Jews, and vice versa.

They had studiously kept Jews out of Palmpoppiesfontien, knowing full well that invasion by that gifted race would soon put them on the streets. Officially they minuted that discrimination against Jews was in the public interest. In fact they knew that there was not a lawyer, doctor, accountant or businessman who would survive against their meanest Jewish equivalent.

Morison gathered his wits about him, not liking to have his aplomb shaken. 'But why must we now allow Jews in?' he asked. 'We have already agreed that we will remain in control of the influx.'

'Och mon, use yer heed! We'll hae to admit companies galore when the toon starts tae grow. Hoo can ye ken that the XYZ company is not Jew owned or controlled? An' what's tae stop a Christian from sellin' his licence tae a Jew?'

While all the others were dumbstruck by this logic, Mayor Bisley was not going to surrender his dream that easily. He was going to be Mayor of Bisleyburg even if he had to be circumcised himself.

'Gentlemen, I don't disagree with the doctor. This is one thing we shall have to face. If Jews and prosperity go together, then we must accept both or none. Other people have managed to live with them. Why not us?'

'*Nee*, not a damn,' growled van der Watt. 'I'm not voting for any boom or change of name or any damn Jews. If the rest of you do, I'll resign.'

'Accepted,' snapped Morison.

'Huh?' The big man was shocked.

'Come on now gentlemen,' Bisley uncapped the oil bottle again. 'Let's keep this meeting formal. What about a show of hands on these points? Who is in favour of a change of name?'

All hands except that of van der Watt went up.

'And who agrees that we'll have to admit Jews?'

The same hands went up, with the exception of Heinz Gruber who was now completely out of his depth.

'What's the matter, Mr Gruber? Are you abstaining?'

'What have the Jews got to do with the name of our town?' he asked with a worried frown.

They all sighed and Bisley clapped a hand to his brow. Morison quickly pushed the boat back on course. 'Well, it seems that we must change the name of the town, encourage the boom and allow all types into town in the general interest of all concerned.'

'Even Catholics?' asked Lappies frowning.

'I don't see how we can exclude anyone,' said the Mayor. 'All we can do is to make things as difficult as possible for Jews and Catholics and other scum.'

'The town will go to the dogs,' growled van der Watt. 'The day we see a Catholic church built here and a Cohen & Cohen in the main street, we'll know that's the end of us.'

'Nonsense,' snapped Bisley. 'Things may be a bit unpleasant but just think of the money we'll make before the newcomers can find their feet.'

There was a general lightening of the gloom. 'Now, as far as a new name is concerned,' he continued, 'I suggest that we each submit a typed, unsigned summary of the position, together with our choice of name and our reasons therefore. We can meet again tomorrow and discuss the suggestions. Agreed?'

There was a murmur of assent, even from van der Watt, who had no intention of being forced off the council. Now that a renaming seemed inevitable he was going to have a great deal to say therein. Mentally he rolled Wattsrus and Wattsville around his tongue, trying them for flavour.

They rose and filed out of the room. Outside the town hall they went their various ways. McTiver hurried diagonally across the main street and eagerly entered the bar of the President Hotel.

Chapter 2

Sarel Labuschagne, the man responsible for the emergency meeting of the Palmpoppiesfontein Town Council, the expected wave of prosperity, and all the excitement, was suffering.

At sixty years of age, *Oom* Sarel was one of the fittest men in the Orange Free State. Biltong lean, strong as fencing wire, Sarel had never spent a day in bed in his life, had never caught a cold or a disease of any sort. He ate anything and everything and still bewildered his wife, *Tante* Bessie, with the force of his sexual needs. Evidence of this latter potency was scattered all over the Free State and Transvaal in the form of six mountainous sons and four well-married and highly reproductive daughters.

Oom Sarel now lay muttering in bed in a position in which he could not remember ever having had only bedclothes beneath him. The indignity and enforced idleness were rapidly raising Sarel to a state of volcanic fury. The nurses were becoming scared of him and the doctors were eagerly awaiting the day when, as the senior registrar said, 'the old bastard gets his arse out of here'.

His rump had been brought into hospital as a result of the big discovery which, among other things, was supposed to make Sarel a multimillionaire and Palmpoppiesfontein a thriving metropolis. The discovery had taken place a few days earlier on Sarel's farm, Boomplaas, about ten miles out of town. After supper on that fateful day *Oom* Sarel, as was his custom, had wandered down the path to the *kleinhuisie* at the bottom of the garden. The edifice had recently been placed over a new hole, the old one having accommodated its full quota.

Picking the last bits of Bessie's very excellent *bobotie* out of his teeth, Sarel had lowered his pants and relaxed with a sigh in anticipation of a peaceful bowel movement.

He took out his well-loved pipe and pouch of coarse tobacco and carefully rubbed the tobacco into the bowl. He applied the first match and achieved a bit of a glow onto the tobacco before the match went out. The second match soon set the smoke flowing well and Sarel reached behind him and dropped the burning match into the hole.

That was the last thing he remembered for some time. There was a violent explosion and a blue tongue of flame burst out of the hole. Oom Sarel, together with the wood and iron structure, was blown through the air and landed a few feet away, unconscious and face downwards in a position he was to occupy for the next few weeks. His buttocks were seared and impregnated with splinters of timber and other substances.

Tante Bessie, knitting quietly in the *voorkamer*, heard the explosion and rushed to the rear window. With horror she saw the blue flame leaping over the void where the *pragtige nuwe kleinhuisie* had stood.

She rushed out of the house and found her motionless husband on the path, his backside sticking up in the air peppered with foreign bodies and looking something like the pincushion she used when dressmaking.

'*Here, O Here, my man is dood!*' she exclaimed, dropping to her knees beside the still figure. She felt for his heart and soon discovered it beating strongly. She put her ear to his face and was reassured by his strong breathing. Rising, she rushed back into the house and wound the handle of the telephone feverishly. A startled operator said, '*Ja Tante? Hoekom is tante so haastig vanaand ?*'

Bessie did not try to explain but gasped out the gory facts which must have curdled the operator's blood, and yelled, '*Kry vir my dokter Bezuidenhout, niggie, gou gou.*'

It took Corny Bezuidenhout some time to put together a semblance of what sounded like facts from the distraught Bessie and when he set out for Boomplaas he was still unsure as to what he was going to find on his arrival. It all sounded a bit fantastic to him, what with lavatories disappearing, peppered buttocks and flaming gases from the ground.

When he arrived at the farm he took in the clinical situation at a glance, although the nature of the flame escaped him completely. He cleaned the rump and applied a temporary dressing. Then he gently laid Sarel on the back seat of his new BMW gritting his teeth at the possible effect on the new cloth upholstery.

He drove straight to Bloemfontein and handed Sarel over to the mercies of the hospital doctors who were to curse Bezuidenhout roundly for the next few days.

On the way home Corny wondered (a) what the strange flame could be and (b) how much he could charge Sarel for the round trip, including a whack for dry cleaning his car seat.

The sight and sound of the roaring flame had been an unnerving experience. Corny, tired after his long drive and peed off at the state of his new car's rear seat, headed directly for the President Hotel bar on his return to Palmpoppiesfontein.

As expected he found his partner propping up one end of the counter. Angus did not appear to have reached that stage where his pronunciation and comprehension had been reduced to nil, so Corny joined him and began to tell him the events of the past four hours.

Angus interrupted him. 'Yew shtink!'

'Yes, I know, Mac. Sarel was covered all over with it.'
'Did th' aul bassard fa' in then?'
'No man. I'm telling you there was an explosion that blew him and the *huisie* yards away and cut his buttocks to ribbons and now there's this helluva flame coming out of the cesspit.'
'Wash he bin eatin' ter fart li' that?'
'Oh Mac, you're bloody impossible.'
Angus chuckled gleefully and threw an arm around his young partner's shoulders.
'Dinna worry, mon. I foller ye weel. What'll yer charge Sarel?'
'About a hundred rand should do it.'
'Aye. Le's ha' a drinkie on it.'
A tall young man sitting near them at the bar had been following their conversation with interest. He rose and moved closer to the two doctors and extended his hand.
'Good evening, gentlemen,' he said pleasantly. 'My name is William Mortimer. Would you have a drink with me?' He signalled to the barman. Corny shook his hand and introduced Angus and himself.
'Pleased to meet you, Mr Mortimer.'
'Whusky, thanks Bill.'
'I hope you don't think me rude, but I couldn't help overhearing your conversation.' Mortimer addressed himself to Corny. 'I gather you are doctors?'
'Correck. Th' bes'!' McTiver was trying to get his mouth and the glass to meet at a mutually acceptable point.
'I am very interested in this explosion and flame that you were talking about.'
'And what would your interest be, Mr Mortimer?' asked Corny.
'I am a geological engineer attached to SPUDS, that is the Society for the Promotion of Underground Discoveries. I am staying here overnight on my way to Jacobsdal.'
'Shakobsdal? I shpose shome aul hairyback hash crep inna hole wi' a lass an' dishcovered shex an' yuure a goin' to luuk inna it?' Angus cackled again and pounded their backs, slopping whisky indiscriminately.
Mortimer smiled uncomfortably at Corny, raising one eyebrow. 'Actually they've found a large deposit of asbestos there. But I must say I am most intrigued by this flame of yours. Do you think it would be possible to arrange for me to see it?'
'Of course,' replied Corny. 'I'll phone *Tante* Bessie in the morning and tell her you're coming out.'
'Thanks very much. Perhaps you would give me the directions?'
Corny did the necessary and added: 'I'll probably be out there

myself during the day. I should see how *Tante* has recovered from the shock and tell her that Sarel is in good hands. It must have been a damn frightening experience for her.'

'I'll bet she's a' o' a dither aboot Sarel's balls,' slurred McTiver. 'If he's lost those, they'll do theysel's in.'

'I think Sarel's injuries are confined to his buttocks, Mac,' said Corny, getting a little tired of Angus.

'Guid. Noo le's hae a dram fer th' rood.'

Corny was not fooled. The one for the road always came at the time when Angus felt the need to lose himself totally in the bottle. This was usually around 10 p.m. and between then and closing time Angus would reduce himself to a slobbering mess that had to be carried out to a car and driven home.

He ordered the drinks and then turned to the stranger. 'What do you think this is, then, out at Boomplaas?'

'Well, it's impossible to say with any hope of accuracy, without seeing the flame and investigating the surroundings. It may be merely a pocket of natural gas and if this is the case it will burn itself out in a matter of days. But it could mean that there is oil there.'

'Hell!' said Corny. 'Imagine what that would mean.'

'It has been suspected for some time that we must have oil on this subcontinent but generally the geological formations do not correspond with the oil-indicating formations in the northern hemisphere.

'We at SPUDS think it is wrong to presume that there is no oil in this part of the globe. We know that very little oil has been discovered in the southern hemisphere, other than South America, but it is the word 'discovered' that is important.'

'Hell! If there's oil on Sarel's farm we'll be in for a boom,' yelled Corny.

'Drinks all round,' he shouted to the barman and the barflies crowded up to the rail.

'I think that you should be a bit more cautious, doctor,' said Mortimer quietly. 'Even if there is oil there it may be insufficient to warrant viable exploitation.'

'How do you find out?'

'First a full geological survey and tests. If these are positive a few test holes may be necessary.'

'How long will all this take?'

'It all depends. I might be able to give you some estimate tomorrow after I have seen this hole and the flame.'

Within a few days, Mortimer's carefully worded statement, mildly hopeful of finding oil due to the favourable indications, had grown into a Declaration of Independence of the Arabian oil deposits.

The arrival of the top SPUDS man from Johannesburg and his concurrence with Mortimer's opinion fanned the flame of hope into a gusher fire. The populace began to regard the proposed test holes as channels through which new prosperity would flow into everyone's pockets.

The town was gripped in a fever of excitement. Some inhabitants hastily erected 'Estate Agency' signboards with their names and addresses appended, determined to cash in on any newcomers arriving with wads of cash and looking for Klondike land.

The local representative of the Receiver of Revenue had the time of his miserable life doing the rounds of the self-styled agents, extracting a R25 default fine from each of them and forcing them to take out the necessary general agent's licence as well.

Other residents, perhaps more imaginative and do-it-yourself inclined, began to dig up their gardens in search of other signs of black gold. Many put 'For Sale' signs on their homes and sat back arguing with themselves concerning the asking price of their property.

When a breathless Corny Bezuidenthout dashed into Bisley's dispensary and told him of SPUDS's hopeful verdict, the Mayor had trembled with excitement and hastily summoned his council to an emergency meeting.

But everyone was doomed to undergo an excruciating period of inaction. Frustration was etched on the faces of all. Corny had to do an emergency operation on one avaricious old buzzard whose gastric ulcer had been unable to stand the strain and had burrowed through his tripe.

The inaction was due to the facts that:

(a) Sarel Labuschagne's land held the oil;

(b) Sarel Labuschagne was in hospital; and

(c) Sarel Labuschagne would not discuss the matter with anyone.

The old farmer showed no enthusiasm at all when the great news was flung at him by no less a personage than the Mayor himself who had travelled to Bloemfontein expressly to congratulate Sarel (and to do anything else that could be of possible benefit to himself) in the execution of his civic duty.

Labuschagne's feelings, in sympathy with his backside, were still badly hurt by the ignominy of his accident and the impossible physical position in which he was being forced to spend about two weeks of inactivity. Any reference to the explosion, oil or no oil, boom or no boom, was taken with a large measure of umbrage and bushy eyebrows raised above a purpling face.

The twice daily ministrations to his rear and the gusts of girlish giggling in the corridor drove the old man into a red blur of rage which pulsed through his bum like a river in flood.

So, while Sarel fumed and fulminated in the hospital, the townspeople of Palmpoppiesfontein fretted and fidgeted. People began to look sideways at each other with expressions of distrust and all new faces were surveyed with a mixture of greed and speculation.

Chapter 3

At last the going became too tough for *Oom* Sarel. He could not lie another minute in hospital. His progress had been spectacular, due to his excellent physical condition as well as the almost feverish efforts of the staff to 'get the old bastard out of here'.

When Sarel decided to discharge himself from the hospital he was only a few days in advance of the doctors' D-Day and his departure caused them very little professional discomfort.

The same could not be said for the young probationer nurse who popped into the ward 'to see if the old gentleman is comfortable' to find him prancing around the floor, stark naked, tearing open cupboards and drawers in search of clothing.

'Mr Labuschagne!' she yelped. 'What are you doing?'

'I'm going home, *meisiekind,* where are my clothes?'

'B..b..but you can't. Not until the doctors release you.'

'To hell with doctors girl. I knows when I is fit.'

The nurse cast an apprehensive glance at the patient and, with another yelp, hurried out.

By the time she returned with a doctor Sarel had found his clothes and he was almost fully dressed with the bandages on his rump stretching his pants to give him a posterior like a Bushman in mid summer.

'Well, Mr Labuschagne,' said the doctor heartily. 'On your way I see?'

'*Seker, dokter.* There's *niks* the matter with me now. An' I'm getting sick of all these young girls messing around with my backside. *Tante* Bessie will be able to do this much better without being so cold and funny about an old man's private parts.'

'As you wish, Mr Labuschagne, if this is your decision. You should stay another week but if you wish to sign yourself out you cannot be stopped.' He crossed his fingers behind his back.

'*Goed*! An' where's the *telefoon?*' he snapped.

'After he had spoken to somebody at Boomplaas to arrange transport home, he signed the forms that an enthusiastic doctor explained to him and then went out and sat in the shade of a jacaranda tree to await the arrival of his car. The air was warm and scented by blossoms. The effort had tired him more than he would have admitted. The seat was comfortable ...

'No man. Not like that. You'll cut the sheep's tongue!' Old Piet

Labuschagne's spade-like beard waggled in excitement and young Sarel quickly moved the dosing pipe to the side of the sheep's jaw. Kleinbooi poured the medicine into the funnel at the other end of the pipe and the sheep kicked and squirmed in anguish. After its mouth had been held tightly closed for a while it was released and ran bleating to join the other sheep on the far side of the pen.

Sarel stood up, straightening his aching back as the two young black men dragged in yet another protesting sheep and rammed it tightly between his knees. Old Labuschagne nodded his approval and pointed the stem of his pipe at them as he shouted: 'Only sixty more!' Sarel groaned and forced open yet another mouth. Finally, the last sheep rushed into the huddle across the dusty pen and Sarel could stretch his back properly. Kleinbooi picked up their equipment and called his young assistants to drive the sheep out to pasture. Sarel clambered wearily onto the cross bar of the pen next to his father.

They sat in the silence which deepened around them as the men drove the sheep out of the pen and away to the distant camps – a silence that became almost tangible as the sun reached down for the Trompsburg. As the light softened from a metallic brilliance to a golden radiance, it seemed to perfuse everything.

A flight of hadedas headed swiftly for the bluegums near the distant river. Their squawking calls seemed to drift softly down to earth through the thick yellow glow. The old man heard his son sigh softly.

'You love this place, my son?'

'What a question, Father. Who could not love it. Can there possibly be a better place to live?'

Labuschagne chuckled wryly. The beauty of the setting sun and the soft light did much to relieve the stark treelessness and dust of the farm. To love its ugliness as he and his son did, one had to have true farmer's blood.

'My boy, this is but a small place. It is poor and it is bare. It can support only a few hundred sheep. But it is all we have. It is all we managed to save from the English in the War.'

'But it is home, Father.'

'It is yours, Sarel.'

'Of course, yours and mine. It is our home.'

'I do not mean that, son. Now, as of this moment I give it to you. The house, the sheep, the land, all are yours. You are farmer Labuschagne.'

'*Myne? Ag, nee Pa!*'

'Yes, Sarel. It is not often that the youngest son inherits the farm, is it? But you are the only one left. If your brothers had not been killed in the War, I suppose you could not have inherited it. But I think it is right that you should have it. To speak thus of the dead is not good, I know, but none of your brothers had your love of the land and the beasts. None of them would have cared for our little farm as you have done and will continue to do. Now it is yours in fact.'

'But, Father, you are not yet ...' Sarel trailed off in confusion at what he had nearly said.

'Dead? Not yet dead?' his father finished for him. 'No, my son. Don't be upset. Why must Vlakte have two masters? Let me sit here and watch you dose your sheep. Let me perhaps walk beside you as you plough your lands and sow your mielies. Let the sheep know your hands only.'

'I have run my course. Since the War I have lost heart. The only joy since that evil time has been your birth. Then, when God in His wisdom took away our mother, my light faded badly. You are now twenty years old. You are strong and healthy – all that I am not.'

He waved an arm, encompassing all the lands of Vlakte.

'This is not much, but it is all I have to give you. Take it and love it and it will reward you as I wish I could have done.'

Sarel could not force any words past the lump in his throat. But even if he could have spoken, he would not have known what to say. They slid off the fence and walked slowly toward the house.

It was only a house, not a home. At the far end of the sitting room was their reminder of Ma, the homemaker. An oval walnut frame around a fading picture of a black haired, clear eyed woman. There was a half smile on her lovely face, her white lace collar on a plain black dress came halfway up her long graceful neck. Her hair was pulled severely back into a bun behind her head.

She had died in the year the picture was taken, in the great epidemic which swept the globe after World War 1, when Sarel had been fifteen years old.

In the five years since her death nothing had changed on the farm Vlakte and yet nothing was the same. For old Labuschagne the flame had gone out of his life and out of the life of the farm. Dust had settled in the corners of the house, never to be disturbed; weeds had appeared in the garden where formerly they had never dared show themselves.

The two men sat down at the table and a maid brought their supper. After a short prayer they ate quickly and in silence. Sarel's father pushed away his plate and lit his pipe.

'You will marry soon, Sarel?'

'If Bessie will say the word, yes.'

'Good. I will only go in peace when I have seen my first grandson.'

Sarel blushed slightly.

'My son, you must have responsibility to give meaning to your work. You must work for a reason and what better reason can there be than the preservation of your own line?'

'Yes, Father.'

'Then go to Bessie and her people. Go now. Tell them that you are a man of substance. Set the day and make your old father happy for what is left of his life.'

Sarel slid his horse to a halt outside the Van Lingen's house, noting with relief that there was a light on in the sitting room.

He entered to find the family gathered around the huge oaken table. Bessie's father, a patriarchal figure very similar to Sarel's own father, sat at the head of the table with his huge gnarled hands on an open Bible. Opposite him sat his wife, *Tante* Sarah, while Bessie and her five sisters and brothers filled places on either side of the table.

'Good evening *Oom* Hannes, *Tante* Sarah,' Sarel said breathlessly. 'I am sorry to interrupt the prayers.'

'You do not interrupt them, *seun.* We are about to begin. You may join us. Sit there next to Bessie.'

Sarel drew up a chair next to her and Van Lingen began to read. He read well and the beautiful resonance of his voice and the High Dutch phrases filled the room in praise of God.

For the first time in his life Sarel was impatient with prayers. He began to fidget and Bessie laid her cool hand on his arm and looked at him sternly out of the corner of her eye.

After the reading, Van Lingen closed the Book gently and began a long rambling prayer which included all members of the family and relatives to the fifth degree, living and dead and for what appeared to be the last fifty years. For good measure he threw in the names of all friends who came readily to mind.

When at last he ceased Sarel felt as if he were about to explode.

'Young Sarel has the impatience of a *rinkals* tonight,' Van Lingen said kindly. 'He has news of great importance?'

'Yes, yes, *Oom* Hannes.' Sarel stole a quick look at Bessie, who looked mystified.

'Is it something we may all know, or is it only for the ears of our Bessie here?' he said with a twinkle of mischief in his eye. He chuckled when he saw both his daughter and Sarel blush.

Sarel could contain himself no longer. 'I am a farmer, *Oom* Hannes!'

Van Lingen was unimpressed. 'So you are, and a very good one at that. I too am a farmer. So?'

'*Oom* Hannes is being difficult. I mean I am a real farmer.'

'But surely we are all real farmers. This is our life, not our pastime.

You sow your mielies, you dose and shear your sheep. So do I ...'

Sarel interrupted him with a gesture. 'But I now own Vlakte. Today Pa gave me the farm. I own it all.'

'But the house lacks a wife, no?'

'Ag, Hannes,' chided *Tante* Sarah, 'you tease the boy too much. Sarel we are so happy with you and we know you will always be a good farmer.'

'Oh Sarel, I am so glad,' exclaimed Bessie.

Sarel gathered his breath and looked at the expectant faces around him. He swallowed.

'Mr Van Lingen, I come to you tonight as a man of means, seeking your permission to ask Bessie to marry me.'

Despite the fact that their eventual union had been as pre-ordained as the rising of the sun, the announcement galvanized them all into action as if it had been a complete surprise. They crowded around Bessie and Sarel, kissing them and crying and laughing.

'Wait!' Van Lingen's command stilled them. 'I have been asked, but have I replied?'

'Hannes! You can surely have no objection,' Sarah gasped.

'No,' he replied slowly, 'I have no objection.' He stressed the last word and Bessie and Sarel looked perturbed.

'I have no objection, granted, but I do have a condition to impose.'

'Anything, *Oom* Hannes, anything,' said Sarel.

'If Bessie is to marry you, you are immediately to plant ten trees for each member of our two families and add another ten for every child and grandchild until you die.'

'This is a strange request, *Oom* Hannes, but I will do it with ease.'

'Then you may ask my daughter to marry you.'

Sarel turned to Bessie and took her hands in his. 'Bessie, my treasure, will you marry me?'

With a look of annoyance at her father, Bessie replied, 'Of course, Sarel, I will marry you as soon as you say the word, trees or no trees.'

Van Lingen glanced at his wife and raised his eyebrows, a grin forcing its way to his lips. 'Our daughter has her mother's spirit.'

He turned to Sarel. 'My request is not an idle one, my boy. I have for many years been concerned at the barrenness of our veld. Now, trees bring the rain. It is not the rain that causes trees to grow. This is a complementary thing between the clouds and the earth and the trees. Where there are trees there will be rain. Where there is rain, there is a prosperous farmer. If you are that farmer, my son, then my daughter and my grandchildren are well protected. So you see, my condition is no idle thing. Further, as your wedding present I will order for you one hundred saplings from the nurseries in Bloemfontein.'

'*Oom* Hannes, thank you. And I think it will also be right for me to rename my farm. From now on it shall be Boomplaas.'

'A very sound idea, Sarel. Now, before I pronounce my blessing on this betrothal, let us decide on the wedding day.'

'The week of *Nagmaal* in October,' said Bessie without hesitation.

'But that gives us only two months in which to prepare,' wailed *Tante* Sarah.

'Then we shall have to work quickly, won't we, mother,' replied the girl with finality.

With another shrug at his wife, Van Lingen stood up and raised his hand over the heads of Sarel and Bessie. His prayer was full of faith and hope and this time Sarel listened eagerly.

When at last Sarel and Bessie were alone, she patted the couch next to her and said: 'Come. Sit Sarel. We have much to discuss and plan.'

She looked up in surprise as her man shook his head.

'No, you plan and do what you will. I have a farm to attend to. Tomorrow I start the holes for the trees.'

He kissed her goodnight and strode out to his horse.

With pride, Bessie remembered that night for the rest of her days. That night he had set the pattern of their life together. His was the man's work, the farm and all that went with it; hers was everything else.

Sarel let his horse walk home. The early spring night was clear and the air crisp. The moon was three quarters full and in its pale light Sarel could see his land – his land – stretching away towards the Trompsburg. At the foot of the mountains was the river, but this was not in his land. Not yet, he thought. This would be his first objective – to extend his lands right to the river and maybe the mountains.

Van Lingen's words and his own father's echoed in his mind: 'Trees bring the rain'; 'responsibility makes a man'.

In his mind's eye he could see groves of trees clustering around the homestead and stretching away in lines and groups to link up with the bluegums near the river.

He would plant medium-sized shade trees near the house and would line the farm road to the highway with poplars. Closer to the river he would plant large trees where their roots would draw on the underground water and not drain the fields of their moisture, which was needed for the mielies.

When he extended his farm the new camps would be laid open to sheep. The trees near the house would make his home an oasis in the desert of the Free State.

Bessie would help him.

He stopped his horse in the dusty yard behind the homestead and looked around: not a bush, not a shrub, not a tree. The patch of vegetable garden that his mother had tended so carefully was a jungle of weeds and the great sweep of lawn across the front of the house was a sandy patch of blistered roots.

Men had no time for such things. Certainly men on their own had no time. With Bessie there, the homestead would again flourish.

He walked his horse to the stables and put it up for the night, thinking that a few shade trees around the outbuildings would be a great improvement.

In the house, he stood for a long minute in front of the picture of his mother. Pale in the moonlight that filtered through the windows, she seemed to smile sweetly at him.

'She will be worthy of you, Mother,' he said aloud and went to his bedroom.

He went to sleep trying to remember all he knew about trees and dreamt that he was planting trees with Bessie beside him. Then, suddenly, he was very old, strangely old, and he was sawing through the trunk of a thick bluegum tree as old as himself. Bessie was shaking him and shouting: '*Moordenaar, moordenaar!*'

He awoke with a start and saw his beautiful granddaughter standing over him with a firm hand shaking his shoulder.

'Really, *Oupa*,' she was saying. 'The sound of your snoring will wake all the patients in the hospital. How can an industrious farmer sit and sleep in the shade of a tree all day when there is work to be done?'

Sarel straightened up, rubbed his hands across his eyes, ran his tongue around the inside of his dry mouth and yawned.

'Yes, Tina,' he mumbled. 'Come, my child, drive your sick old grandfather home to Boomplaas.'

As Tina turned the car off the main road and headed up the drive of poplars, Sarel looked at the nameplate fixed to the gateposts: Boomplaas.

He remembered his recent dream and how, forty years before, on awakening the morning after his visit to the Van Lingens, he had crept out of the house and quickly shaped a piece of timber on which he had painted the name, Boomplaas. Then, going down to the entrance, he had removed the sign, Vlakte and replaced it with the one he had made. After breakfast he had asked his father to ride down to the gate with him, where he had pointed with pride at his handiwork.

'Boomplaas?' the old man had said. 'But there is hardly a tree on the whole farm!'

'I know, Father, but soon there will be many.'

Then he had told his father the events of the previous night. His father's joy had been wonderful to see and when the old man, to hide his tears, had suggested gruffly that they go and select some suitable places for planting, he had agreed with alacrity.

'*Kom, Oupa,*' Tina said. '*Ons is nou tuis.*'

Sarel realised that the car had stopped outside his house and Tina was holding open the car door for him.

He climbed out stiffly and walked slowly into the coolness of his and Bessie's home.

Chapter 4

That afternoon Sarel decided to take a stroll over the farm. He set off in a very good mood, relaxed after his homecoming celebration with *Tante* Bessie. He wandered around the base of a little *koppie* and was startled to see a young man on his knees examining the ground carefully.

'Hey, *jong*,' he bellowed, 'what you doing hey?'

The stranger scrambled to his feet and dusted his knees and hands. He grinned at Sarel who thought this was quite a good looking *outjie*.

'Good afternoon,' said the young man. 'I'm William Mortimer.'

'An' so?'

Spuds looked a little blank. 'Well, er ... um ... I'm ... er ... the chappie who has diagnosed the presence of oil on your farm.'

'An' what you doing now on your four feets like a dok?'

'I think this is a likely spot for our first hole. The surrounding formations point to a high peaked fissure about a thousand feet down. I think we'll find a healthy pocket of oil right below our feet.' He smiled happily.

'Oh. Izzatso hey? An' what makes you think there's going to be holes dug all over Boomplaas?'

'Good heavens, Mr Labuschagne, surely you realise that we have to drill holes to get the oil out of the ground?'

'But who says you can take out the oil, hey?'

'I..I'm afraid I don't quite understand you, Mr Labuschagne. Surely you don't mean that you are not interested in the oil?'

'I do.'

'You aren't even interested in becoming a millionaire?'

'Listen, *jong*, I don't care nothing for money. I've got plenty an' lots of farms an' all my children is well fixed up. Now, why must I make Boomplaas full of holes, just for someone else to make money out of my farm as well?'

'But just think how famous you would be and how proud you'd feel that you had given such prosperity to your town and something so vitally important to your country.'

Spuds began to get worked up.

'To see Boomplaas covered with towering derricks, reaching for the sky but drawing up from under the earth the life blood of your country!'

'Hey, who is this Derek chap?'

'No, no, Mr Labuschagne, derricks. Big towers that are erected at each hole for the drilling and pumping out the oil.'

'WHAT! Blurry poles an' things all over my farm too as well as holes! *Nooit!* Not a damn. I think you must bugger off now.'

Sarel's excitement increased his blood pressure and his injured rump began to throb. Spuds was dismayed.

'B..b..but Mr Labuschagne ...'

'*Ag, nee wat.* Youse not such a bad young chap, but nobody is going to make a helluva mess of Boomplaas. *Kom,* let's go an' have some of *Tante* Bessie's *lekker koffie* an' then you can go home.'

The old farmer set off briskly and Spuds hurried after him. As they came within hailing distance of the homestead Sarel started yelling for coffee.

Entering the house behind his host Spuds was blinded by a vision of loveliness that rose from a chair and undulated towards them. She was about twenty years of age, as blonde as Miss Sweden and twice as lovely.

'Hullo, *skattie,*' said Sarel and turned to a transfixed Spuds. '*Boet,* meet my granddaughter. Tina, this is Mr Williams Mortimer.'

Spuds felt his hand clasped in a cool grip and his eyes drawn into twin pools of purple that twinkled at him from a height of only about five foot three inches.

'Hullo, Mr Mortimer.' Her voice was like a delicate silver bell.

'M..M..My friends call me Spuds,' he stammered, holding on to the hand firmly.

'Spuds. What a strange name,' she said with a smile and cocking her delightful head to one side.

'You see, I'm the oil man,' he said lamely and reluctantly gave her back her hand.

'But I thought you *Engelse* called potatoes spuds,' she said with a very straight face.

'Oh, no. It's an acronym – the word is made up from the initials of other words. Like this: S-P-U-D-S.'

'And that means oil?'

Sarel was enjoying Mortimer's discomfort but he thought it was time to rescue him. He knew just how the young man was being churned up inside. It had been like that when he had first met Bessie. She had been a girl just like Tina. Not showing as much bare arm, leg and breast, of course.

'Man, Tina,' he said. 'This Spuds is the man who wants to dig holes all over Boomplaas and bring in David to pump out the oil.'

'Er ... derrick ... Mr Labuschagne,' corrected Spuds.

'Ag well, *wat ook al.* But I want no holes or oil an' no more money either,' he added quickly to pre-empt that argument.

'Do you really think there is much oil here, Mr Spuds?' asked Tina with a smile that made Mortimer's knees jellify.

'Just Spuds..er..Tina. Yes, I do. If the deposits are in accordance with the indications of the tests, there is a fortune to be made out of Boomplaas.

'But, as your grandfather doesn't want any drilling on the farm and has no wish to make any more money, it will remain locked up in the ground until someone else controls this farm. Someone who might be more interested in the progress of this area and the good of the country.'

For a moment he thought he had gone too far, but Sarel relaxed and grinned. He liked this *outjie* who liked his Tina. And he did not like people to be scared of his temper.

'Man,' he said happily, 'then you're going to wait a helluva long time to *pomp* oil out of Boomplaas. I've got plenty of sons to carry on an' they've already got sons to follow them. An' I'll make sure they'll treat this beautiful farm just as I do. Oil must come from the Arabs, mielies and sheep from Boomplaas.'

'But *Oupa*, there are lots of other farms,' said Tina. 'You could make yourself a lot of money and turn this into a very rich and important area and then buy yourself another farm. A bigger, better farm even.'

A raising of the bushy eyebrows evidenced rising anger, despite it being the wonderful Tina who was involved. 'An' just where is there a better farm than Boomplaas?' he asked thickly.

Just then *Tante* Bessie came in followed by a maid bearing a huge stinkwood tray laden with mugs, a pot of coffee and a vast pile of *koek-susters*. She poured and the sacrament of coffee was received with due reverence.

Spuds poured coffee down his tie as he tried to drink while feasting his eyes on the vision of Tina, daintily biting a *koeksuster* and sipping her coffee prettily.

Tante Bessie was telling them of a new recipe she had discovered and which was at that very moment in course of preparation for the evening meal, when the arrival of a car was heard outside followed by the slam of the front door. Corny Bezuidenhout came into the room, complete with bag of tricks.

'So it's true, you old kudu. Got sick of hospital eh? I can't say the doctor who phoned me from Bloemfontein sounded very sad to see the back of you. Why must you be so difficult?'

'They weren't as pleased to see me go as I was to get the hell out of there. *En daardie verpleegsters. Magtig!* The worst of women. No shame, no decency, no sympathy for an old man in pain. No respect for his private parts.'

'Don't make me laugh. I can't think of anyone less interested in sympathy than yourself. Anyway, I've come to have a look at you and check your dressings. Where's your room?'

They went off down the passage and *Tante* Bessie went back to her kitchen. Spuds looked at Tina. Tina looked at Spuds.

'Do you live here, Tina. On the farm, I mean?'

'No, I live in Palmpoppies,' she said. I drove up to Bloem this morning to fetch *Oupa* from the hospital. Mr Morison gave me the day off.'

'Who's Morison?'

'He's a lawyer in town. I work for him.'

'And your parents?'

'They have a farm in the Western Transvaal. My father is *Oupa's* eldest son.'

'But why do you live and work here, then. Why don't you go to Johannesburg?'

'Well, *Oupa* is so happy to have me near him, so I thought I'd work for a few years here, getting experience, and then I'd go to the big city when I'm twenty one. I've lots of old school friends here, but it would be lovely to live in a big city.'

'Palmpoppiesfontein will be a big city one day soon, you know.'

'Because of this oil?

'But *Oupa* won't let them take it out!'

'I'm sure he'll see reason soon enough. Perhaps you could help to convince him that it's the right thing to do? He thinks the sun divides its rising and setting places between you and Boomplaas.'

'Maybe. But you know, he'd be very hurt if he thought I didn't think as much of Boomplaas the beautiful as he does. That I could even imagine all those holes and douglases on the farm would be incredible to him.'

'Derricks, Tina.'

They laughed together and then Spuds asked: 'When are you going back to town?'

'Just now,' she replied. 'Why?'

'I thought we could go back together in my car,' he said hopefully. 'Perhaps we could have some dinner together and you could tell me all about yourself and your interesting family and town. I would like to get to know as many people here as possible and I'm not moving on until this oil business is settled.'

'That would be lovely,' she said brightly, 'but I'll need more than one evening to tell you all that.'

Chapter 5

The Mayor regarded the collection of envelopes on the table before him as would a mongoose a cobra. The councillors sat around the table, palms flat on its polished surface, and looked at him in silence. All except Gruber wore their best poker-faces.

Van der Watt looked like a newly castrated bull and Drumpel like a St Bernard that had lost its cognac in the snow. Lappies LeRoux resembled a constipated ferret and McTiver, screwing up his face and battling to focus his eyes, bore a striking resemblance to a caged monkey trying to inveigle a spectator into passing the bananas.

Completely bewildered already, Heinz Gruber's sick grimace was frightening in its inanity. The only one who could muster up a true deadpan was Morison. Professionally he had found it advisable to cultivate a bland expression, both for leading unsuspecting cross-examinees into traps and for acquainting temporarily relieved clients of his fees. He leaned back in his chair, fingertips together, a slight smile tickling his lips as the Mayor's hand hovered over the envelopes.

Full of a sense of occasion, Bisley cleared his throat and said: 'Gentlemen, this is an historic moment. We are gathered here to debate in all seriousness the future of our town and to make a decision, the first of many no doubt, that will, we hope, prove to be the right one for the furthering of the town's prosperity and that of all its inhabitants.

'When, beginning with the farm Boomplaas, the surrounding areas yield their treasure and the wave of prosperity gathers, we must be ready to deal promptly with all the demands that will be made on us as administrators of this town. We must adhere to our principles and support each other loyally and, above all, we must be able to debate effectively all trading applications put before us and do this in a spirit of team work for the good of the town, putting our personal interests behind us.'

He saw Morison's sardonically raised left eyebrow, but he plunged on valiantly. 'Let us bend our minds objectively to this, our first task of historic importance.'

Gesturing at the envelopes before him, suddenly resolute, he picked up one at random. He opened it and, unfolding a small scrap of paper, perused it in silence.

'Well, read it out man,' bellowed van der Watt in frustration. 'How the blazes can we discuss and vote on something we know nothing about?' His jaw threatened to dislocate itself without further notice.

With a bewildered look on his face, Bisley stopped squinting at the paper in his hand and, whitening with suppressed anger at van der Watt's rudeness, threw the paper at him saying: 'You read it out yourself. I can make neither head nor tail of it.'

Van der Watt took the paper and adjusted his spectacles. He squinted and screwed up his eyes and turned the paper upside down. It was not typewritten, but scrawled in a shocking hand and in what seemed to be a foreign language. He shook his head and passed the paper on to Lappies who took one look and shoved it on to Heinz. He snatched it up joyously and leapt to his size thirteen feet.

'Ag! Sats *mein* baper. *Ich bin* ze winner!'

'What the hell are you shouting about?' demanded Morison crossly. He grabbed the offending paper and waved it angrily. 'You must be mad! Stark staring raving bloody mad. We can't even read it. And what have you won, anyway?'

'Sats *mein* entry. *Mein* comes furst ze pile out, so I'm winning. *Ek's* got ze choosing from our new name.'

Mayor Bisley grabbed his overheated brow. He could see that the next big administrative project was going to be getting this idiot off the council and back to his grease bay where he could do relatively little harm.

'Mr Gruber,' he said patiently, 'this is not a game of chance or a competition. This is a serious discussion of how to rename our town in keeping with its new growth potential. Have you by any chance in your..er..entry form indicated what you think that name might be?'

'Ja, Ja, *bestemt*!' shouted the excited garage man. 'Sere it is, sere.' He pointed to an ink blob at the bottom of the page, from one side of which protruded 'Jo..' and from the other '..urg 2'.

'What might that signify, Mr Gruber?' Bisley asked wearily.

'Man, can't you read: Johannesburg 2!' Heinz shouted in glee and grinned in anticipation of their plaudits.

The councillors exchanged significant looks. The Mayor grabbed the next envelope and tore it open with trembling fingers. Gruber opened and closed his mouth a few times and then subsided in sulky silence, all his effervescence gone like forgotten Enos.

'The importance of our town's name,' read Bisley, 'must not be underestimated and in choosing a new name two factors must be borne in mind, namely:

(1) the new name's connection with prominent people or current events; and

(2) the nature of our future image.

Bisley stole a quick look around and, seeing Morison's smile, deduced that this was his 'entry'. He continued reading.

'In the first context let us consider (i) people and (ii) events.' Bisley was beginning to look for a few subsections and notwithstandings but carried on happily.

'(i) The name of either our first Mayor or our present one would be a good solution to this aspect of our consideration.'

Bisley squirmed with pleasure. The first mayor, in 1884, had been an oaf named Myles Clarence Bing. History did not tell how this solitary Englishman had got himself mixed up in what was at that time a totally trek-boer community, let alone how he had been acceptable as the first mayor. In any event, his name could not be used in any prefixed or suffixed form so Bisley thought that this subsection of the Morison report pointed clearly to a name like Bisley(burg).

Basking in the speculative glances of his councillors and trying hard not to smirk, Bisley carried on with the reading.

'(ii) Events must have a bearing on a town's name as can be seen in the naming of many of our towns and cities. Cape Town was so named because of its geographic position. Quaggasfontein was named so because of the mass slaughter of *quaggas* there when the Boers ran out of biltong in 1899.

'Now, our own event is the discovery of oil in Palmpoppiesfontein. How can we incorporate this into a name suggestive of the discovery? We have the example of Sasolburg, where oil is made from coal and the Sasol of the name is derived from *Suid Afrikaanse Steenkool en Olie* and their motor registration is OIL. Can we do something similar? Could we name our town 'Lubeville'? That would suggest a connection with lubricants and have a vague similarity to Labuschagne.'

Bisley looked around and was relieved to see expressions of disapproval on all faces, except of course for Heinz Gruber, who may as well have been on Mars for all the empathy he had with the meeting. The Mayor turned once more to his reading.

'Our future image is hard to predict. If we become purely an oil producing area and lose control, the town will evolve into a grubby smudge of untended housing scheme cottages. If a degree of this is unavoidable, our new name must be diametrically opposed to such a picture. Something like 'Arcadia' or 'Virginia' would do.

'If on the other hand, we manage to attract a diversity of industries and are able to control the influx, we can construct a beautiful, well laid-out metropolis. If the poetic thought can be forgiven, I would then suggest a name like 'Oleander' which also has an oily connection.

'To sum up, however, and to cast my vote, I would say that a personage is a more permanent factor than an event and the name of a well-known and well-liked citizen is more meaningful than a synthetic tag.

I therefore suggest 'Bisleyburg' as our best choice.'

Putting the paper reverently onto the table before him Bisley felt a Drambuie-like glow permeating his viscera. His breath whistled through his teeth in relief. His pleasure was almost sexual.

'Well, gentlemen,' he said huskily, 'I think we will all agree that this is a very concise summing-up of the situation. In all humility I must say that if the name is chosen to be a memorial to my small efforts on behalf of our town-becoming-city and a suitable title for our new metropolis, I shall certainly not spare myself in the furtherance of our prosperity. It is a great honour which one of you gentlemen has wished on me and I thank you, whoever it might be.'

His glow was ruined by McTiver who yipped: 'Theer's anuther five o' yon bitties tae see furrst, Bisley. Let's hae a wee luke at th' lot, if y' dinna mine.'

'Of course, of course, Doctor,' said Bisley with a malevolent glance at his arch enemy. 'I do feel however that each of these reports should be acknowledged immediately.'

'Surely you don't expect us all to vote for your ridiculous name, Bisley?' growled Drumpel, coming to life unexpectedly and placing himself squarely as a right-winger. Bisley gave him a withering look and tore open the next envelope. He read.

'It was obviously the foresight of our Afrikaner forbears to settle in a place where their descendants could live in prosperity. We should therefore honour them as our predecessors in the building of the nation. It is a fact that LeRoux was one of the earliest names among settlers in this district.

'I am not writing this myself, but I vote that Mr B A LeRoux, as the direct descendant of the founders of this town, should be honoured by having his name used in the renaming of Palmpoppiesfontein. I suggest Rouxburg.'

Lappies' smile slipped into his lap as six pairs of pitying eyes in six sadly nodding heads, looked steadily at him.

'Really, Mr LeRoux,' said Bisley, self-righteousness oozing from every pore as he reached for the next envelope.

He was just about to start reading the next 'entry' which he recognised as his own, when he was again rudely interrupted.

'Jest a wee minnit, Bisley,' the little doctor was bobbing up and down in his seat. 'Wha' aboot th' discussion on tha' verry guid idee?'

'Yeah!' chimed in the others, except Morison, who was Mona Lisaing at the ceiling.

'Well, gentlemen, are there any comments? It is obviously an attempt by Mr LeRoux to swing the vote in his own favour.'

'An' what's wrong with that?' demanded van der Watt, his protective stand earning a grateful look from Lappies.

'Well, it's not done. One doesn't vote for oneself. We must be objective about things like this.' Bisley's own 'entry' was by now burning a hole in his hand.

'Ag, man!' thundered van der Watt. 'You said yourself that we must look at this matter with the best interests of the town at heart. Lappies has been very brave and honest in suggesting a really sensible name for the town. What he says in his paper is true. LeRoux is certainly an older name around here than Bisley.' He spat out the last word.

'B..b..but he's not even the Mayor,' spluttered Bisley. 'I don't think there's ever been a LeRoux Mayor.'

'Well then, let's make him Mayor. Take off your lavatory chain and give it to Lappies,' van der Watt said happily.

Bisley was still spluttering. Morison came to the rescue.

'An excellent idea, Mr van der Watt, but, I fear, not very practical just at present. Constitutionally the Mayor must be elected by the people, as Mr Bisley was, and his term of office has another four months to run. Should Mr LeRoux stand for office in April, I'm sure he will obtain a share of the votes and, if in the majority, will become the Mayor. As to his suggestion of renaming the town after his ancestors, I think it is a good one and will have to be voted on in due course.'

Shaken, Bisley again picked up his 'entry' and was about to read his anonymous defence of 'Bisleyburg' when the door burst open and a distraught Corny Bezuidenhout rushed in.

Bisley barked. 'Really Doctor, don't you realise that Council is in session, and a very important one at that. This room is strictly private.'

'I'm sorry, Tom, but this is serious. I have very bad news!'

'Sarel's lost his balls!' cackled McTiver, but Corny waved at him impatiently.

'Much, much worse, for all of us. Sarel refuses to sell one square inch of his ground to anyone at any price and says that the oil can stay where it is.'

'Good God!' yelped the Mayor. 'He can't do this to us. Has he gone mad?'

'No, he's quite sane. He says he's got enough money and he likes Boomplaas and Palmpoppiesfontein just as they are and he is not going to turn his ancestors' land and graves into a mess of oil drills and he doesn't want Palmpoppies to become a slum of dirty houses and milk bars and insurance companies.'

'But he must be crazy. He can't stand in the way of a city or a nation's progress. We'll have to go and sort him out.' Bisley's voice had risen to a squeak.

'Och weel, yew due th' sortin' Bisley. I'm a wee bittie dry,' muttered

Angus and he toddled out dragging Corny along with him.

A hubbub broke out as the rest of them began to jabber excitedly. Mayor Bisley banged furiously on the table until the outcry, with a final whimper from Lappies, finally quietened.

'Now, gentlemen,' he said firmly, 'let us remain calm. This is a new problem but by no means an insurmountable one. Councillor Morison and I will see Sarel Labuschagne immediately and obtain clarification and the facts for us to debate at a later stage. I am sure Sarel can be made to see reason. This meeting is now adjourned and will continue on the subject of a name when this more basic setback has been resolved.'

The councillors murmured agreement and trooped out in silence, gloomily contemplating shrunken bank balances. The Mayor dropped his head into his hands and stared sightlessly at the polished surface of the table.

As Morison went out he turned to Bisley and said: 'Don't worry, Tom. I've got an idea. I'm going up to Bloem. You see old Sarel in the meantime and try to talk him around, but if you have no success I think I can unearth something to fix him.'

Across the road, in the President Bar, Angus and Corny were already on their second drinks.

'So what,' snorted Corny. 'Bugger the oil. We've got enough tonsils and gall bladders to keep us going for a long time.'

'Aye, le's drink tae that!'

Chapter 6

Bisley absentmindedly dropped two Disprin into his tea and gagged at the first sip. This was driving him mad. He did not like complications. He did not like people to disagree with him. He could certainly not accept what looked like a reversal of all his dreams of wealth and the glory of Bisleyburg née Palmpoppiesfontein.

Something would have to be done about Sarel's nonsense. He couldn't be allowed to sit on the oil mine like a dog in a manger. He wondered what it was that Morison had up his sleeve. As if he didn't have enough to worry about, now he had to deal with a rich old fool of a farmer: a real old *boer* who had made a great deal of money simply through love and knowledge of soil, crop and beast. The fruit of his labours was monetary gain in a world where this was the criterion of everything.

'Well,' he sighed to himself, 'one must start somewhere.' He stood up and removed his chain of office. Then he put on his hat and went out to the waiting Mayoral car.

He told the chauffeur to drive slowly out to Boomplaas. Then he leaned back in his seat to do some constructive thinking as opposed to daydreaming. How do I approach old Sarel? The wrong words at the beginning could foul up the whole operation. Were the hell do I start?

As the car trundled down the main street Bisley looked at the buildings on either side. Instead of the grubby little LeRoux Outfitters, Watt's Deli and the tumbledown bank and building society buildings, he imagined twenty-storey skyscrapers ablaze with neon, and great plate glass windows letting one see everything in the shops as one strolled past. He shuddered at the sight of the President Hotel which still sported a hitching rail outside the main entrance. The Dutch Reformed Church frowned down the main street from a bend in the road. Its twin mahogany doors stood fast in juxtaposition to the happily swinging doors of the President Bar.

Bisley thought that the church would be quite inadequate for the population influx when it came. One thing about these Afrikaners – they were certainly churchgoers. The car passed the Methodist hall which had the capacity of about a hundred and fifty people and a flagpole from which the Rev Travers flew a Union Jack if he ever had a congregation of more than a dozen in attendance. Methodists, of course, could and did worship anywhere. It was not necessary to be led around by the nose by Bible-thumpers every week. The DRC and the

Romans really had their people under the whip. Bloody good for the offertory collections of course.

The car left the town and the veld began to widen out on either side. Then they crossed the surprisingly wide Steen River which curled in a great loop around Palmpoppiesfontein before swirling off to meet the Rietrivier at Koffiefontein.

The Steen was an unusual river, nearly always in motion and, at many places, deep and swift. Occasionally in mid-summer it would absorb great quantities of water from its watershed and rush down to Palmpoppiesfontein. There it would leap over its banks and pour through the lower lying areas of the town, playing water polo with the hysterical inhabitants of the lower income groups. After the floods there would be the Mayoral Relief Fund Appeal and the proceeds, less expenses, would be distributed to the unfortunates.

In March there was the Mayoral Cocktail Party for members of the higher income groups. Last year the floods had been severe and the hearts of the contributing populace had been effectively touched.

Accordingly the Mayoral cocktail party had been lavish. It had been at that party that Bisley and Morison had renewed their pact to keep control of the town to themselves. Also, Corny and Angus had reviewed the progress of their 'operation appendix' and considered the relative merits of gall bladders and prostates.

The car rumbled over a gravel road and Bisley noticed that it was Boomplaas land that now stretched on either side of the road. Soon the car slowed down and turned up a drive lined with poplars in full leaf.

Sarel was sitting on the front stoep drinking coffee. He put down his cup and went out to the car. He opened the door and pulled Bisley out by the hand shaking the hand and Bisley so that the Mayor winced with pain.

'Hullo, ou Tom,' he said, 'how are you, man?'

'I'm fine, Sarel, thank you, just fine,' Bisley replied as he surreptitiously worked his shoulder back into its socket. 'But how are you? Surely you're out of hospital a bit too soon?'

'Yirra man. I couldn't stand those nurses another minute. They nearly drove me mad. An' there's nothing wrong with me now. Just a few bandages to fix now and then.'

They went up onto the *stoep* and Sarel handed his guest a cup of coffee. Bisley sipped it and, mentally squaring his shoulders, got down to business.

'Corny tells me that you are not all that pleased about oil being found on your farm?'

'Hell, Tom. Would you be pleased to be blown up in a lavatory?'

'No, of course your experience has been most unpleasant but surely you are excited that you could soon be the owner of the biggest oil business in the country, maybe in the southern hemisphere?'

'*Nee,* man. I'm *sommer* a *boer.* What do I know about oil?'

'But, Sarel, you don't have to know anything about oil. All you have to do is sell someone the mining rights for a hefty cash payment and a percentage of the production, so much a barrel, and then you sit back and become a millionaire.'

'An' then they come and bugger up Boomplaas, cut down the trees, kill the veld, drive away the animals and dig holes for Derrik all over the place. An' if they don't find enough oil they yust go away and leave Boomplaas opgebogger for me to plant more trees and fill up the holes. *Nooit!* Never!'

'Sarel, young Mortimer is absolutely sure that there is a huge oil field here and that expert from Johannesburg confirmed it. Boomplaas might be spoilt a little, but certainly not without reward.'

'No, Tom. Boomplaas is a farm, not an oil well. I'm happy to leave it so.'

'Then what about Palmpoppiesfontein, Sarel? Do you realise that you have it in your power to turn our town into the biggest city in Africa? You could become the richest and best known man in South Africa. Don't you think you owe this to your country, let alone your town and district or yourself?'

'Would you like to be mayor of such a big place, *ou* Tom?' asked Sarel blandly and Bisley looked at him keenly but could see nothing suspicious in the smiling biltong face.

'I hadn't thought about that, Sarel. It's beside the point anyway. If I didn't want to be mayor, I'm sure there are plenty of people suited for the job.'

'So you wouldn't worry if someone else was mayor when Palmpoppies got big?'

'Good heavens, no, Sarel,' said Bisley uneasily, not liking the drift of the conversation. 'But we are getting away from the point. As Mayor at the moment I have a great duty to the town, which is why I am so concerned at your attitude. You are wanting to block the prosperity of us all and keep our town a *platteland dorp* forever.

'I quite see your side of the picture and appreciate your concern for your lovely farm, but I do feel that you should be looking at the greater good of the greater number. I honestly think that you should sacrifice your own love of this farm in the general interests of the community and what is more, your country.'

'Now you are trying to make me feel like a traitor or something?'

'Well, Sarel, that is the opposite of patriot. If you sacrificed your farm for the good of the country that would be a great act of patriotism.'

'So, not to let them cut my farm to bits would be a traitor's doing?'

'You said it Sarel.'

'Now you make me think, Tom.'

'I'm glad, Sarel. I don't think that anyone would expect you, or any true farmer, to relish the idea of mutilating his lands and turning his fields into an eyesore. You can't take such a decision without a great deal of thought. But I know you will think about this honestly. I just hope that you will see it from the point of view of Bis.d.. er Palmpoppiesfontein.'

'OK then Tom. I'll think about it. Have some more coffee.'

There was a lull in the conversation while they slurped at their cups.

'How's that fine granddaughter of yours these days, Sarel?' asked Bisley, peering over the rim of his cup.

'Man, she gets more *pragtig* every day. Just like Bessie was forty years ago.'

'Rory Morison tells me she's a good worker too.'

'That's good. Your Mr Mortimer also thinks she's something,' said Sarel with a wicked glint in his eye.

'Why do you say **my** Mr Mortimer?'

'Well, he found the oil for you, didn't he?'

'No, **you** found it, for all Palmpoppiesfontein!' Bisley gestured expansively with his free hand.

'Ag man, all right. But he is the one who wants to bugger up my farm.'

'But not your bank balance.'

'Nor my granddaughter.'

'Eh?' Bisley was shocked but the old farmer burst into gales of laughter.

On the way home Bisley toyed with the idea that the old chap was possibly certifiable but he couldn't work out just how this would help them in the current campaign.

After Bisley had gone, Sarel walked across his lands in the yellow light of the reflected sunset and climbed to the top of the little koppie near the spot where he had found Spuds.

He sat down carefully and filled his blackened old pipe. In the distance he could see a flock of sheep coming slowly towards him. Far away on the left, at the base of the mountains where the river turned and approached the town, he could just make out the dark patches of green maize, already six feet high.

He was sad. In his heart of hearts he knew that Boomplaas would have to go. He also knew that it could never be replaced, not in what was left of his life, anyway.

Of what use would more money be to an old man who would not even be able to sit on his *koppie* and watch his sheep coming home and his mielies growing near the river and the sun setting over the mountains.

In town, at the President Hotel, Spuds was enjoying a cool shower. Fresh lightweight clothes lay on his bed. In half an hour Tina would be at his side. They would have dinner as they had the night before, then another drive to the grassy river bank where they would look at the moon in the sky above them and in the water below them.

In her room, in the home of one of her many aunts, Tina stood naked from her bath and critically surveyed herself reflected in her full-length mirror.

She thought of Spuds and the moonlight on the river and grinned at herself as she felt and saw her nipples rise stiffly on her firm breasts.

Chapter 7

Angus McTiver opened one eye and shut it quickly as the subdued sunlight behind the bedroom curtains tore through his eyeball and seared the back of his head.

Keeping his eyes closed, he worked his thick tongue away from the top of his mouth, then he felt around on his bedside table for a glass of water, a little of which slightly reduced the parrot's cage of his mouth.

He turned over slowly in the bed, facing away from the window, and slowly opened the eye again. It stayed open so he opened the other. He lay quietly, gathering himself for the effort and the inevitable pain of getting up and taking those few tottering steps to the shower.

He wondered why he couldn't adapt better to drink and its side effects. In more than twenty years of boozing on an ever increasing scale, he had never been able to acquire any measure of tolerance or the morning ability to wake up, get up and get going. Surely, he thought, one's body should get used to grog in twenty years.

Angus loved booze and it really did not seem to disagree with him, organically that is. But he had never been able to avoid or cure the hangover. He thought it a worthwhile subject for research. The trouble was, who the hell was going to do the research? No one knew the miseries of a hangover without experiencing one, and no one in the throes of one was in a position to be clinical about it.

One couldn't put one's headache and nausea under a microscope. And no amount of aspirin or bismuth seemed to have any favourable reaction. The only relief was that first drink of the day, while the extreme anxiety of waiting for it was the worst suffering of all.

He was determined that he would not drink before ten a.m. He was not an alcoholic. He was whatever the nicer word for drunkard was. If he had to drink on awakening he would have to classify himself as an 'alkie' and that was not on.

He could not subscribe to that drivel about it being a disease. In his weaker moments he wished he **could** call it a disease and let himself float away on waves of alcohol and self-pity while legions of white-coated people all over the world strained to find a cure for it.

At first he had been able to last until lunch before having his first drink. Now, more from the desire to relieve his misery than anything else, he allowed himself to start at ten a.m.

He was beginning to feel as if he could make it to the shower when his wife opened the door and walked in. She had her own room. Angus' nightly condition made his presence in her bedroom undesirable from the point of view of rest and marital relations.

'Angus, don't you think it's time you got up?'

'Aye, Beth. I'm gettin'.'

'Your tomato juice and toast are on the table my dear. I'm going down to the market.'

Angus shuddered, even though it hurt his head. Tomato juice! His stomach would take nothing until after a few whiskies and then it would only handle dry biscuits.

He clambered wearily out of bed and dropped his pyjamas to the floor. His white, wrinkled body mocked him from the mirror. Twenty five years ago, what it had lacked in size, it had made up in power and endurance. Ruefully he thought the same applied to his sexual organ.

He had been a champion lightweight boxer and a powerful swimmer. His lack of height had affected his service, but otherwise his tennis had been devastating. His few seasons of rugby had shown him to be a first class scrum-half. Then, at twenty five years of age, freshly qualified, he had been sucked into the maelstrom of the Second World War, which had spewed him out, still a doctor deft and experienced in emergency, but on the crest of an alcoholic wave that reared itself above what seemed to be a bottomless trough.

From practice to smaller practice in the cities, to work in the country, to emigration, to GP in South African towns and finally to Palmpoppiesfontein, had been his unalterable fate, prescribed by the moving finger of the first barman who had chalked up Angus' first drink.

Now his once hard flat stomach bulged and hung sadly, his biceps were wrinkled and his thighs thin. His penis had pointed only at his toes for years.

He shuffled off to the shower and, summoning all his willpower, turned the cold water on full. Three minutes of this left him feeling clean and more alive, but the headache banged away inside, made even worse by the onslaught of the needles of cold water.

He dried himself slowly, leaning his head on the cool tiles of the shower cubicle. He was sitting on the edge of his bed, fully dressed at last and thinking about venturing out into the blinding sunlight when Elizabeth returned from the market.

'I stopped at Mr van der Watt's shop, Angus dear, and bought you some lovely kippers. Wouldn't you prefer them to the tomato juice?'

Elizabeth McTiver had character: she was tough. She was not ready to give up. She had married Doc Mac during the war and even then he had been drunk. From then on it had been a battle between the bottle and herself for her husband's affections. At first it had been possible to combine sex and booze. Now she was definitely the loser. But the Battle for Angus would go on.

Each and every day there was something to try, a possible break-through to her bewildered husband. It could be a new idea, a new dish, a holiday plan, contract bridge. Not for nothing had she been the matron of a large military hospital and her organisational ability produced plans of attack in a steady stream.

'Noo thanks, Beth,' he restrained another shudder. ''tis tae soon a'ter th' grog tae eat. Fer supper they'd be guid.'

Beth knew he'd no more eat the kippers at supper time that he would eat them then. He wouldn't even be at home at supper time.

'Mrs B. told me at bridge yesterday that there was some snag with this oil business. *Oom* Sarel doesn't want to sell, or something?'

'Aye. Th' aul bassard is medieval. Not tha' I'm no enjoyin' tae see the slug squirm.'

The slug referred to was Bisley. There was no love lost between the chemist and the doctor. Ever since the day Angus had prescribed some medicine for Miss d'Olivera, a highly respected descendant of some Original Inhabitant and whose reputed virginity had by now irrevocably put an end to the d'Olivera blood line.

Angus had prescribed for her at a time when his inebriation necessitated prudent self-effacement. The script had intrigued and amused Bisley who had accordingly sent Miss d'Olivera a harmless concoction with a note saying that he was unsure as to whether the medicine was for her or for a pregnant fox terrier and that before consuming the remedy she should check with her physician.

The resulting furore had been majestic in its intensity and three-cornered threats of libel action filled the air. The matter had come to a mystifying and rather farcical stop when the d'Olivera fox terrier, supposedly spayed, had suddenly swollen up and dropped a litter of five pups, much to the shock and disgust of mama and the delight of the townspeople. The incident rankled and McTiver and Bisley hated each other in a frighteningly civilised way.

Angus explained to Beth how Bisley was pushing the oil boom, supposedly for the good of the town, but of course with a very high degree of self interest.

'It's as plain as the nose on his ugly fiz tha' he's after namin' the toon fer hisself an' bein' th' mayor till he's daid!'

'Angus!' Beth spluttered as a plan of attack *par excellence* struck her so forcibly that she gasped.'

'S matter, Beth?'

'Angus, just imagine! Just imagine how it would ruin old Bisley if you were made mayor!'

Angus snorted. 'Noo, who wuid imagine me a mayor?' he asked with something very close to self-pity in his voice. Beth immediately pounced on his wistfulness.

'Angus, let's give it a try. Oh, how I'd love to be mayoress of Palmpoppiesfontein.'

Her enthusiasm and her longing ignited the blue touch-paper of hope that had been flickering in McTiver's mind for some days. Why not? If that idiot can be a mayor I can be a better one. If this oil business does get going, that moron Bisley won't be able to cope and the town will start looking around for a more competent one. Me!

He bludgeoned his stomach back into line and said briskly: 'Beth, le's start reet noo. I'll hae th' kippers a'ter a'.'

With her feet six inches off the floor, Beth hurried away to the kitchen as Angus poured a handful of aspirin down his throat, straightened his tie and marched purposefully into the dining-room.

It was a startled Corny Bezuidenhout who arrived at his consulting rooms at nine a.m. to find his partner *in situ* and seven surprised and satisfied customers already on their way to collect their medicine or to shave their pubic regions and present themselves at the cottage hospital.

'Mac! What the hell are you doing here?'

McTiver glared at him balefully over the top of his spectacles.

'Earnin' me keep, boy. An' wha's more, dinna let me see yer creepin' o'er the rood tae th' President a' tea time. Theer's wurrk tae be doin'.'

Considering the possibility and cost of psychiatric treatment, Corny stumbled off to his rooms and abstractedly began his morning's work.

Chapter 8

Heinz Gruber wiped a greasy hand across his face leaving a black smudge across the bridge of his beaky nose. He straightened up from the engine of the car on which he was working and flung a spanner onto the workbench.

Rebellious thoughts forced themselves through the clogged passages of his brain as he remembered the cavalier treatment he had received at the hands of his fellow councillors at the last meeting, especially that pompous Bisley.

To think that he had considered them friends. It had seemed that they were on the occasion when he had seen ruin staring him in the face when a big petrol company had opened a garage and filling station in the main street. By some juggling in high places they had managed to get the council's ruling against their licence application reversed at Provincial level and had joyfully poured R250,000 and six ultra-modern petrol pumps into their project.

They started handing out free sweets and cool drinks to the kids and seat cushions to the motorists. The tankers had to start calling very often to replenish the underground storage tanks.

Heinz had howled to the council and they had quickly passed an amendment to the by-laws making the entrances to the new garage's driveways illegal because now the road required full guttering at precisely those points.

The few motorists who remained loyal to the new garage soon got sick of bumping their cars over the kerb to get to the pumps.

The oil company had retaliated by putting extra long hoses on their pumps and serving their customers at the kerbside, but this was doomed to failure by impracticality and the council administered the *coup de grace* by declaring a no stopping zone outside the premises.

Eventually the oil company washed its hands of Palmpoppiesfontein and on their departure sold their building for a fraction of its cost to someone bidding on behalf of Gruber himself.

In his disillusionment with his colleagues, Heinz Gruber remembered the words of his long-departed father, who used to give them a pep talk on their claim to aristocracy at regular intervals. 'Heinz, *mein* zun, *orlwais* gemember sat ve har frum Shermany aus. Ve are moch better bepple san sese half an' half dogs. Sey is shust munkrels; ve are of pure Sherman plud, not mit uzzer sorts of plud upgemixt.'

Apparently such pure blood is also prone to clotting at unexpected times for Gruber senior had collapsed and died as a result of a severe coronary thrombosis at the age of forty eight, leaving Heinz the sole owner of his flourishing garage. The business had prospered in Heinz's hands. He was a good mechanic and spent a great deal of time working on the vehicles himself, a fact which kept him well supplied with satisfied customers.

Once, Heinz had decided that he deserved a holiday. He and his family motored down to Durban and boarded the Oranjefontein bound for Hamburg. Full of excitement on arrival, enjoying the prospect of a meeting with his aristocratic grandparents, they hired a taxi and gave the driver the address.

He was surprised to note that the car travelled through increasingly shabby surroundings and, when it finally stopped, he found himself outside a shack that his black domestic in Palmpoppiesfontein would have scorned.

The meeting with the grandparents was difficult and, escaping as soon as he could, Heinz rushed his family away from their roots and feverishly spent money, forcing out of his mind the vision of the two raddled old beings from whom he had sprung.

Fear of disclosure about his background hung like the sword of Damocles over him, especially when he had acquired the important position of town councillor. His wife had been warned of a fate worse than death if she in any way disturbed the myth of the Gruber aristocracy.

He went cold when he thought of how Bisley and the rest of them could make capital out of the truth. With the new era dawning, he, Heinz Gruber, must remain fixed in the eyes of all as an essential cog in the administrative machine. There was no reason why he shouldn't run for mayor himself.

He stood in the sun outside his lubrication bay and basked in the mayoral dream. He had no doubt that Bisley would sort out the immediate problem. It would be clever to let Bisley do all the spadework and then run for office himself.

He would dish out free petrol for a whole week before the elections. They would be bound to make him Mayor.

Chapter 9

Felix Drumpel gazed out of the window behind the Mayor's head. He could see the bend in the river and he watched the brown wavelets swirling up against the bank and leaping for the fingers that the willows trailed towards the water.

Bisley's voice droned on and on about their present and their future. In a matter of two weeks he had moved from being merely a pompous ass to an incredible bore. All he could talk about was the oil and the expectation that Palmpoppiesfontein would become the pulsating heart of the oil-bearing basin of South Africa.

Despite the fact that for the present Sarel Labuschagne had quashed all their hopes and plans, Bisley went on and on about the forthcoming development and the parts they were each going to have to play in the industrial boom.

Felix was essentially a practical man. What could be more practical than the disposal of the dead? He saw no sense in the oratory of the Mayor. He saw no purpose in these interminable meetings that would be all the more senseless if Labuschagne remained firm in his no oil attitude.

Practical questions like, 'what are you doing to influence old Labuschagne?' met with a marked lack of enthusiasm from Bisley who, when pressed, confused them all, except Morison, with a flow of long-winded euphemisms that defied the comprehension of such humble men as undertakers, drapers, grocers and mechanics.

Bisley had reached the point where he was reconstructing the town's traffic arteries. He was artistically executing a two-handed description of the flyovers and bypasses that would be necessary when Drumpel, identifying with the hardened expressions of his colleagues, suddenly allowed his exasperation to boil over.

'Mr Mayor, for God's sake, what are you doing about the oil?'

'Oil? Doing? Me? Really, Mr Drumpel, do you expect me to go and pump the bloody stuff to the surface myself?'

'You know just what I mean, Mr Mayor. Here you are creating a city that depends on the whim of some crazy old *mielieboer* but what have you done to change Sarel's attitude? How can you continue with all this airy-fairy planning if you can't even tell us that Labuschagne is being made to see reason? You are asking us all to run before we can walk.'

'Mr Drumpel,' replied Bisley heavily, 'I should have thought that you would display more confidence in the person of your Mayor. You surely do not think that I would lead you into discussions of our city-to-be if I was not certain that the smaller problems were under control?'

'So Sarel has agreed to the oil pumping?' asked van der Watt, working his jaw furiously.

'Well..no..er..not exactly ...'

'Then how can you say you have the matter under control?' yipped Lappies.

'Ja. Furst tings furst,' brayed Gruber, immensely pleased that he had grasped the gist of the exchanges. He basked in the glances of approval from his colleagues.

'Noo, jest a minnit,' said Angus, 'le's heer what auld Tom has ter say. Jest hoo far hae ye gone tae talk Sarel aroun'?' he asked Bisley.

The Mayor threw a look of distaste at his enemy. He liked the little Scot's patronising attitude no more than he liked the disturbing rumour that Angus was off the bottle. Despite his weakness, McTiver was well liked. Any turning over of leaves by Angus could well put the axe to Bisley's tree.

'The position is, gentlemen, that I have visited Sarel and discussed the question with him at great length. I have pointed out to him his duty to the town and the country. I have appealed to his patriotism and attempted to sting him into conscientious thought. I am sure my urgings will bear fruit.'

'And if not?' rumbled the council *en bloc.*

'Well..I..um..er..I can't see him refusing.'

Morison rose majestically to his feet and smiled his evil smile at them.

'Gentlemen I am ashamed of you and your lack of faith in Mr Mayor Bisley. Your narrow outlook, your preoccupation with trivialities amazes me. I promise you that I intend to do all in my power to ensure that our new city, whose birth, despite your childish doubts, is imminent, will have its affairs handled by men of greater vision than is evidenced here.'

The gathering looked at the lawyer in amazement. They knew the power and the menace of the man and that he could not be trifled with.

Lappies whimpered quietly as he felt the phantom chain of office slipping from his narrow shoulders. Van der Watt looked into the side streets of a metropolis, teeming with supermarkets, and saw himself dismally slicing bacon in an ill-lit cubicle of a shop, far removed from the heady air of public office.

Felix suddenly felt as cold as one of his corpses.

'Yes, gentlemen,' continued Morison, 'you have shown yourselves to be lacking in that prerequisite of successful administrators – call it big match temperament if you wish – to cut through all the padding and reach and deal with the crux of the problem. I can but hope that the inevitable influx of businessmen will provide some mentalities more suited to the office which you now hold.'

He gazed at them malevolently for a pregnant few seconds and then continued. 'To satisfy your childish fears, however, and to assist Mr Bisley to continue his visionary approach to our golden era, I will tell you that I have the means to force Sarel Labuschagne to relinquish his dog in the manger attitude. The weapon I have is not one that I would like to have to use and I will not unless Labuschagne remains adamantly against developing the oil.'

'Blackmail?' they chorused in delicious horror.

'Certainly not, merely a matter of law which I do not propose to discuss here and now. If it is not necessary to use it, then it will never come into the open at all.'

There was a sigh of relief from the assembly. Bisley looked quizzically at Morison. He knew nothing of this secret weapon and hoped to hell that Rory was not chancing his arm.

The councillors settled themselves lower in their chairs as Bisley, with renewed vigour, launched once more into his oration, his flow of words increased now by his new confidence.

He became a Moses viewing from the Land of Bondage the transfluvial Promised Land. But, unlike Moses, he was determined that he was going to be the first to sink his tin mug into the milk and honey. He was not going to be buried on a hillside overlooking the Land of Plenty to which he had unselfishly guided his people.

Felix Drumpel's face grew longer and longer. The prospect of teeming throngs of people, living out their precious few days before succumbing to his inevitable ministrations, made him morbidly happy. Business would be good.

He was not so pleased with the drift of the Mayor's harangue. He was more observant and intellectually endowed than his colleagues and he began to realise that Bisley was talking himself into an unassailable position of authority wherein his dictatorship would be unchallenged. He also began to sense the amount of self-interest that pervaded Bisley's vision.

There is no reason, he thought, why this man should take all the glory. It was quite accidental that Sarel had struck his match during Bisley's term of office. There was nothing to guarantee Bisley's continued rule after the next elections due in April.

Sarel might have struck his match in May, when even he, Felix Drumpel, might have been Mayor. Even poor old Heinz Gruber might have been wearing the chain of office and throwing the Percentage of Flood Victims Relief Fund party.

Chapter 10

Tina looked up from her typewriter as Spuds strolled in looking very cool in a white safari outfit.

Morison's office was situated in a side street, just off the main thoroughfare and the window behind Tina afforded an excellent view of the river. The view was enhanced by the cool green of the trees and the lush grass near the river bank, which also served as the town's public park, except during the 'monsoon'.

To the right and almost out of sight at the top end of the town, one could see from Tina's window the high bank and the bend of the river as it turned away from the town.

'Good morning, Tina.' Spuds had a naughty grin on his face.

'Hullo, Willem.' Was that a slight blush?

'Working hard?'

'Oh, yes, there's always a lot to do here.'

Spuds wandered around the desk and glanced pointedly up the river. Tina followed his gaze and felt her cheeks redden and her nipples push against her clothes.

She was wearing a thin cotton blouse and, to her consternation, she saw that her nipples were projecting boldly. Spuds' grin became broader and even more suggestive.

'Willem, you are a bad man!'

'Last night you told me I was a darling. Does this mean that you're not going out with me tonight?'

'Not there!' She jerked her head towards the river.

'Oh?'

'No. We're going to the farm for supper. *Oupa* wants to see us.'

'What about?'

'It must be something to do with this oil.'

'Have you said anything to *Oom* Sarel about it?'

'No. I'm scared of saying the wrong thing.'

'Well, we'll just play it by ear this evening. Is your boss in?'

'Yes. You want to see him?'

'You don't think I came here just to see you.' She put her tongue out at him and motioned him towards the door of the inner office.

Spuds knocked and entered. Morison was standing behind his desk, hands behind his back, gazing out over the river. He turned to his visitor and greeted him, gesturing to a chair before sitting down himself.

'Mr Mortimer,' he said fruitily with a man-to-man air, 'thank you for coming. I asked you here to discuss this topic of general interest in which you find yourself the central figure.'

'The oil or Mr Labuschagne?' asked Spuds warily.

'Or even his granddaughter,' chuckled Morison greasily.

Spuds looked questioningly at the lawyer. 'The whole matter seems to be at a standstill anyway. No one will be able to get things moving except Mr Bisley and Mr Labuschagne.'

'My boy, I don't think Bisley can do very much. Sarel is a stubborn old goat. I think something more than plain persuasion is going to be necessary. But, before we adopt any sterner measures, I would like to see this impasse settled amicably.'

'Naturally,' replied William, feeling a lot less calm than he sounded. He found his dislike of Morison growing with every smooth word that slid from the fat lips.

'The facts are that the town must not be deprived of this opportunity to develop. Sarel must be induced to agree to the exploitation of the oil, by whatever means we may have to use. The end, in this set of circumstances,would always justify the means, but, before we 'pull out all the stops' as it were, I want to appeal to you, on behalf of the Mayor and the council, to do all you can to substantiate this great vision that lies before us.'

'Well, Mr Morison, of course I intend to do all I can to see that this find is developed. This is my job, my duty to the Society, irrespective of any wish I might have on behalf of Palmpoppiesfontein.

'The trouble is that I can't see any way in which I can do any more than anyone else the way things are right now. Once Mr Labuschagne gives the word I can move very quickly, but I certainly can not see myself talking him into anything where you and Mr Bisley and his other friends have failed to move him.'

Morison looked steadily at the young man. 'My boy, you don't realise just how much you can do. If you knew how much regard Sarel has for Tina you would realise what a powerful weapon you have. Entice the girl onto our side and induce her to work on the old man. It will be for the good of all.'

'Yes, I see no problem there. However you must remember that Tina is extremely fond of her grandfather; she wouldn't do anything to hurt him. She knows just how much Boomplaas means to him and she is very worried that she might say the wrong thing and make him feel that she is against him and the farm. I have discussed this whole business with her and she does agree with me. But blood is thicker than oil, you know.'

Morison laughed. 'Well said. But I am sure that you can do a great deal to help us and under very pleasant working conditions as well, I might add.' His smile was full of meaning and Spuds was quite sure he did not like what he inferred.

He rose and said, 'I will do all I can.'

On his way to the door, he stopped and turned around. 'You indicated that there were other means by which you could force *Oom* Sarel to his knees. What precisely?'

'Better that you don't know my boy. But don't worry. Everything that we have in mind is perfectly legal and above board.'

Spuds had a feeling that this last remark did not ring true, however he kept silent. Tina smiled up at him as he closed Morison's door.

'My, but you look serious, Willem.'

'This is a serious business, Tina.'

'What is?'

'Loving you,' he said unexpectedly and went out without another word leaving her all thumbs on her typewriter.

They sat close together as the car carried them out of the town, across the river and into the lands encircling Boomplaas. Tina thought that the invitation from Sarel was unusual in that, because Sarel expected them to, people were in the habit of calling in at any time, with no reason other than *geselskap.*

It was evident that *Oupa* had something on his mind. It did not need a great mind to work out that it concerned the subject of oil, Boomplaas and Palmpoppiesfontein.

Tina was worried about the coming discussion and resolved not to hurt *Oupa's* feelings for any reason whatsoever. But she was also aware of the common good and the need for prosperity.

Mortimer's problem was similar and complicated by the fact that it was his duty to promote the interests of SPUDS. What was worse was that in arguing strongly with Labuschagne it was quite possible that he might upset Tina. She would defend the old chap like a lioness with cubs.

He decided that it would be best to play the whole thing by ear in accordance with whatever trend the discussion took. He let his pent up breath out with a snort and Tina glanced at him with a smile on her face.

'What is the matter William Mortimer?' she asked impishly.

'I was just thinking, Tina, that this is becoming a messy business.'

'Do you think that *Oupa* should let them take the oil?'

'I wouldn't be a good member of the Society if I did not, but I can certainly see *Oupa's* point of view.'

'Oh well, don't worry,' she said innocently, 'if he really doesn't want you to have his oil, you can just go and look for it somewhere else.

Surely Boomplaas isn't the only place in the country with a bit of oil?'

'There may be oil elsewhere,' replied Spuds thickly, 'but there will certainly not be another Tina.' He leaned over and kissed her. Due to his inattention the car started running off the road and he corrected it quickly.

They drove the rest of the way in silence.

When they arrived at the homestead, *Oom* Sarel was waiting to meet them and, as the car drew up, he came down the steps shouting a greeting. Then, walking between them and holding an elbow in each hand, he walked them up the steps and into the cool house.

Tante Bessie was, of course, in the kitchen, from which direction came mouth-watering smells. Sarel fussed around like a hen and when he had settled William, he brought out a bottle of brandy. Tina refused a drink and said that she would go into the kitchen and see *Ouma.*

Spuds saw a tumbler, half filled with brandy, plonked down on the table before him. He was relieved when his host asked him if he would like some water with it and replied that he thought it might be a good idea. Sarel grabbed an enamel jug and tipped a thimbleful of water into the glass.

They toasted each other and drank. Spuds was glad that it was twenty year old KWV, smooth and mellow. He could get it down without losing his breath and gasping. He was sure that this would have been a loss of face in front of Sarel.

The old farmer came to the point with disconcerting directness.

'Williams Mortimer,' he said, 'what must I do about this blurry oil?'

'I was under the impression that you had made up your mind about that, Mr Labuschagne,' Spuds said.

'I had. I don't want to lose Boomplaas, but now this Bisley talks about being a patriot and a traitor. This makes me think that after all an old man still has no right to his land and his peace, for which he has worked all his life. Why can't you go and find some oil where there are no mielies or sheep and the land is not so beautiful that it would be a sin to spoil it with all the ugly things that you tell me must come with the oil?'

'Perhaps we could find other oil, Mr Labuschagne. No doubt there is oil in other parts of the country. But the fact remains that we have found oil here, easily, and in what appears to be highly workable quantities. The fact that it has been found without the usual expense of months of survey and test drilling, makes it imperative that we try to develop it fully. So far it has cost nothing.'

Seeing the amused grin on his host's face, he added quickly,

'Er...except, of course, your own er..er..inconvenience.'

'But do you think,' asked Sarel, 'that if I did not let them cut up my land it would be the act of a traitor?'

'I think 'traitor' is a rather strong word, but there is no denying that, if you did allow them to mine the oil and spoil your land in the process, you would be performing a very great service to your country and town. And you would become extremely wealthy yourself in the process.'

'Ag man,' exploded Sarel, 'I've heard all these things before. Why can't someone give me a better reason for throwing away my years of work? I have lived here all my life. I have seen Boomplaas grow from a smallholding to one of the biggest farms in the Free State. As I bought the farms on either side of my lands I improved them and turned this part of the country into something far more beautiful than it was a mere fifty years ago.

'I have grown to love every koppie, every anthill. This farm has been as much a mother and father to my children as *Tante* and I have been.

'I have felt the droughts as much as the dry earth and the parched beasts and in the really bad years I have cried to see the loosened earth blown over the mountains in a red cloud. And when the droughts have broken I have rejoiced with the lands and the rivers and the trees.

'My ploughs have been the instruments of a good doctor, helping a fruitful woman to bring into the world healthy children.

'I have planted every tree that you see growing here and my own hands have dosed and tended every sheep that you see out there on the lands.

'Now I am being forced to turn it into a black mess of steel and trucks and oil that squirts around and kills all around it. I ask you, young man, what reason can be given to an old man that will help him to kill his love without dying himself?'

'You ask me for another reason, Mr Labuschagne,' said Spuds. 'Perhaps what I have to say can not be called a reason, but it is certainly something that will give you food for thought. Perhaps give you a different approach.'

The old farmer looked at him from beneath his bushy eyebrows and said: 'Go on then, go on. But stop this Mr Labuschagne *twak*. To everyone of your age I am *Oom* Sarel.'

Mortimer took a deep breath.

'Have you ever considered, *Oom* Sarel, that in the lives of all great men there is one outstanding characteristic common to them all? It is nothing but self-sacrifice. I'm not trying to flatter you or to bribe you. I'm not trying to suggest that you go into the oil business to become a famous man.

'I do suggest, however, that a decision to sacrifice your own love of your land would be the act of a great character and the result would demonstrate to the whole country the greatness of such a humble person as a Free State farmer. And heroism is a wonderful example to others.

'Do not have any false humility about this. You are being faced with a very difficult decision and great decisions can only be taken by great men. Even if they make the wrong decision, great men can face their errors and turn their mistakes into success.'

'You speak convincingly, Williams Mortimer,' said Sarel. 'You would make a good *dominee.*'

At that moment Tina returned with a plate of snacks and, hearing the last remark, said with a laugh: 'I wonder if, with his golden tongue, he would have less trouble getting money out of the pockets of his congregation than he is in trying to get this oil out of you?'

She realised her mistake at once as Sarel bristled and turned on her. 'So! You also think that I must ruin Boomplaas!'

Spuds held his breath. This was the moment of truth. Tina stepped forward and, standing beside her grandfather, she placed an arm around his shoulders.

'*Oupa,* you could not be sadder than myself to see Boomplaas die. But I have long ago abandoned this whole business to *die wil van die Here* and I think you should do the same. There are good reasons on both sides of the matter. Both have much right and only God can decide which is the greater good.

'If you are destined to sacrifice yourself and your farm, you will. Don't try to make a decision just because someone is talking to you very convincingly and neither must you refuse to consider the matter because you know that your heart will break if Boomplaas were to die.'

Spuds thought this was a masterpiece of diplomacy but he couldn't help feeling that it was strange how people so often threw their problems at God. They felt that if they called Him into the act and then went ahead, now under His guidance, and made mistakes, then they could blame the whole sorry mess on Him.

Sarel stared down into his brandy and rubbed a calloused finger across his cheek. '*Here,*' he sighed, 'this is a sad day for me. My heart is heavy because it knows better than I will admit that Boomplaas is going to die. But now, let us look at another side of the question. If I decide to let them take the oil and ruin my farm, who looks after it, the business, I mean? What do I know about the oil business? I would sit and watch the town grow and Bisley get rich and all the other sharks getting fat from my oil and all there is for me is a broken heart.'

He drained his glass suddenly, stood up and said: 'Come let's go and see what *Tante* Bessie has for us to eat.'

They followed him into the kitchen where he proceeded to harass his plump little wife by picking up the lids of the pots and poking at the contents with his gnarled forefinger which he licked after each sampling. As he bent over the pots, his damaged rump stuck out sharply in its cocoon of bandages and Tina battled to suppress her giggles.

Eventually *Tante* Bessie shooed them all out of the kitchen and followed them, wiping her hands on her apron. They sat down at the huge table in the dining-room and, after Sarel had said a prayer, *Tante* tugged at a tassled cord that dangled from the ceiling and a maid staggered in bearing trays and plates and dishes of food.

During the meal, Sarel's spirits seemed to revive and he spoke at great length, hardly letting anyone else get a word in. His conversation concerned Boomplaas and farming almost exclusively. Most townspeople and town affairs he dismissed with a shrug and when any particular subject or individual under discussion upset him, he would gesticulate wildly with his fork whether or not it was loaded with food. On a number of occasions when it was, the contents popped off onto the floor and were gobbled up by the dogs which were everywhere on the farm, but which collected under the table at mealtimes.

Sometimes he would stop declaiming and, as his fork was still waving in the air, he would quickly shovel a few peas and grains of rice into his mouth using the blade of his knife, and then carry on talking and spluttering through the food.

When the meal was over and thanks had been given, they returned to the lounge and *Tante* Bessie poured large cups of strong coffee and handed around a dish of her famous watermelon *konfyt*. *Tante* then settled herself beside Mortimer and asked him how long he intended staying in Palmpoppiesfontein. Spuds looked a little uncomfortable.

'Well, *Tante*, certainly at least until *Oom* has decided one way or another about this oil.'

'And if he decides against it?' she asked.

'Then I intend asking my Society for permission to do some prospecting around here on other farms. It is not impossible that the oil-bearing ground covers a large area.'

'So!' snorted Sarel, 'you are determined to pump oil out of this lovely farming land and spray blackness all over the place. You have no feeling for others or the land.'

'No, it's not so, *Oom* Sarel. I have a job to do. The consequences are not really my concern.' He grinned. 'No doubt there are plenty of other places where I could do my prospecting, but I don't think any of them could be as pleasant as here.'

He looked at Tina, who coloured slightly. *Oom* Sarel caught the glance and grinned himself.

'Would you like to be a farmer, Williams Mortimer?' he asked.

'No more than you would like to be an oilman, *Oom* Sarel.'

While he digested this bit of reasonableness, Sarel picked at his teeth with a finger.

'Man, if you're so interested in this sort of thing,' he said, 'why don't you look for water; something that will benefit the farmer?'

Spuds took another deep breath and his life in his hands.

'*Oom* Sarel, all you farmers seem to think that the country owes you a living. Everything must be done for the farmers. Take your own example, water. If I were to divine vast reserves of underground water, who would benefit? Farmer A and farmer B. Yes, of course the whole country benefits if the farmer's output is increased, but basically it is the farmer who cashes in.

'If I find oil or precious minerals, these benefit the entire community, the whole country and surely you believe that if the country prospers the farmer will do so as well. If the country is poor, the farmer will labour in vain, or at least with very little return.'

Spuds could see the veins beginning to stand out on the old man's temples but he was determined to lay this ghost.

'We are always hearing about what the Government is doing to help the farmers. If there is a credit squeeze, the last to get cut back are the farmers. When subsidies are being dished out the farmers are at the front of the queue. When Tom, Dick or Harry goes bankrupt, everyone jumps on him and whips out his share of whatever is left of the poor chap's possessions and assets. When a farmer goes bang, there's a special act of Parliament to protect him, to ensure that boer Jakob lives on to plough another day.

'Yes, *Oom* Sarel, I have the healthiest respect for all farmers. In my job I meet many of them and they are all fine people, but, notwithstanding droughts and all the other natural problems you have to face, I still think that your life is an easier one than that of those who have to battle for an existence in the world of commerce and competition.

'Very few commercial enterprises have co-operative buying and selling organisations to ensure stable costs and guaranteed prices and assured markets, as do the farmers. I respect your profession, *Oom* Sarel. I respect your love of the land in general and Boomplaas in particular, but I could never see eye to eye with all the pampering that the farmer expects and usually gets.'

There was a silence when Spuds stopped speaking. Sarel rubbed a hand across his face, through his hair, scratched in his ear, picked at his nose and looked uncomfortable. *Tante* Bessie quickly switched the talk to recipes and food, addressing Tina and drawing Spuds into the conversation, which soon became nothing but small talk. It seemed to lap around and wash over Sarel, unnoticed.

At ten thirty Sarel said it was time for his dressings to be changed and Tina said that it was time she and Spuds went home.

As the car burrowed its way through the blackness of the tree-lined drive and emerged into the still darkness of the veld night, Tina was silent. Then she said: 'Willem, I think *Oupa* would have eaten up anyone else who spoke to him like that. He must think very highly of you.'

'He is a tough old bird, Tina, but his stubbornness is beginning to annoy me. If I can talk him into giving up the farm, I will do so.'

Sarel lay in the position to which he had by now become accustomed, while Bessie attended to his bum.

'Bessie, *my skat*,' he said sadly, 'must we let them ruin our home? Is this oil really so important? And if we did let them have the farm, where would we live?'

'Surely,' she replied, 'there would be no reason for us to go away? They would not want to drive us out of our house as well?'

'*Nee*, but can you imagine sitting on the stoep on a summer evening and, instead of seeing mielies and the sheep and the storm clouds coming over the mountains, we see only the tin shacks and the trucks and the Douglases that go with this oil business? How do you think I could start to die here and see my life's work ruined, buried under a sea of black. And what could Boomplaas then mean to our grandchildren?'

'I don't know, Sarel, I just know that whatever you want and whatever you do will be the right thing and I will be beside you.' She had to tighten her neck muscles to stop the tears from springing further than the backs of her eyes.

She finished her ministrations in silence.

Chapter 11

The barman at the President Hotel was white with shock and the regulars were aghast. Angus was on his eighth ginger ale.

Corny and Angus had arrived together and when Angus ordered a ginger-ale the barman screamed with mirth and pointed a disbelieving finger at his star customer while his other hand held his quivering belly.

'The doctor is making jokes!' he bellowed, and reached for the Johnnie Walker.

Angus had drawn himself up haughtily to his full five foot six inches and repeated his order. Capitulating with dismay, the barman realised that the takings were going to be down that night. However, he worried unnecessarily. All shock was assuaged by Angus buying round after round of drinks for everyone and keeping pace himself with ginger-ale. It was a changed man who stood in the doctor's usual drinking place and instead of gradually reducing himself to a slobbering mess, rapidly became the centre of attraction and not for his largesse alone.

Angus revealed a sparkling wit and an inexhaustible fund of anecdotes and jokes. He regaled them with stories of things that could only happen to a doctor and thrilled them with his wartime experiences.

The barman forgot the time and when the manager came in to see why the bar was still open, he also became absorbed in the little Scotman's performance and the free liquor.

The party became louder and louder and by now even included the local constable who had originally entered the bar to investigate the flagrant breaking of the law.

Little did they realise, as they quaffed their free drinks, that they were in phase one of the Make McTiver Mayor campaign.

The barman had a parrot which was normally the centre of attraction in the bar due to its ability to use foul language and its capacity for alcohol. Tonight it was ignored and accordingly settled itself in a corner of its cage sulking silently.

Around midnight the party reached the stage where the policeman's helmet was being used to pass around a concoction of beer, whisky, sherry and gin. The cop had been in no fit state to argue when his helmet was commandeered.

Even the parrot was unable to remain in retreat and, becoming inspired by the extreme sociability of the gathering, loudly demanded a bloody drink, which it got, and then began to fill the air with obscenities.

The nights were becoming a major problem to Mayor Bisley. The worries of the day had to take their place among the other activities of a mayor and a chemist during the sunlit hours. But, after the sun had set and the sundowners consumed and the evening meal was over, Bisley found himself unable to read or talk or listen to the radio or do anything other than worry about Sarel and his oil.

It was useless going to bed; he could not sleep. His frustration at Sarel's attitude was increased by his own inability to formulate a plan of attack that would engage the attention of even the most moronic of his councillors.

Neither did it help his frame of mind to know that these same councillors would be the first to climb on to the bandwagon once he had got it going, despite the fact that they were unwilling to try pushing it in the beginning.

'Stop frowning so, Tom,' snapped Agatha jerking her prune-face in his direction. Her knitting needles flashed and crackled at him, devouring an unending worm of primrose wool. She was knitting a pullover for their son, for the winter. This was her duty from which she would not swerve.

The son, Percy, was at university doing, of course, pharmacy. The unfortunate lad, besides having acquired his mother's shrewishness and his father's avarice, was also effeminate, stoopy-tall, pigeon chested and short-sighted.

Agatha's main redeeming feature was that she loved her son with all the protective ferocity of a lioness. She had resisted successfully all Tom's attempts to make something of a man out of the boy. Long ago Tom and Agatha had stopped fighting about money, of which there was plenty; sex, of which there was none; social standing, which was assured; and holidays, which they always took separately. Instead, they concentrated on the battle for Percy.

If he had been able to wander around in his subconscious mind, Tom Bisley would have noticed a striking similarity in all the phantoms that lurked therein – Agatha!

He would not have admitted it, but he had his reason for seeking public office – not altruism, not self-aggrandizement, not even civic duty – nothing but sheer escapism as a relief from the reality of life with Agatha.

But, whereas he had once been a hard-working pill roller, making a decent living in a reasonably pleasant town and returning home to a rather pretty if spoilt and vacant wife, now he had become a dyspeptic self-seeker.

He would have been happy to have seen his son develop into all the things that he himself would never have seen as his lot. He would have been happy to remain just a small town chemist to bask in the glory of a highly successful son.

The impossibility of the dream soon became apparent and Bisley cringed in the sure knowledge that his son would never be capable of perpetuating the name.

'I'm not frowning, Agatha, only thinking.'

'About your oil, I suppose.' She sniffed.

'Yes.'

'I must say I've never seen you worry as much in all our married life. I would have been very happy to see you worry this much about your family. And for you to be so completely beaten by an old fool of a farmer is nothing short of laughable.'

'What do you mean, 'beaten'?' he asked.

'Well, that dirty old Labuschagne has you all running around like a bunch of beheaded fowls in your attempts to get your hands on the oil rights. He's loving every minute of it and playing hard to get, just to make sure that when the selling time comes it will be at his price, not yours.'

'Really, Agatha, you don't understand the first thing about this. No one is trying to buy anything from Sarel and he's not actually being asked to sell anything. All we want is for him to allow some private enterprise to take over the mining rights on his farm. None of us will be involved in any financial way but eventually all of us and the whole town will prosper.'

'Huh!' she snorted. 'I can't see you and old Morison and the rest of your vultures sitting around quietly while all this prosperity is divided equally among all. You'll be right there at the head of the queue.'

'And I suppose you will be at the head of another queue dishing out money to your favourite charities,' he said sarcastically.

Her needles clicked and clacked a little faster.

'No, I shall continue putting aside every penny that I possibly can for Percy, a duty which you, as his father do not appear to have recognised.'

'Don't be daft, Agatha. Percy isn't going to need all that much money. When the time comes there will be this flourishing business here for him to walk into.'

Agatha dropped her hands and knitting into her lap and looked at him aghast.

'You don't mean for one minute that you think Percy is going to come and waste his life in this silly little town just as his poor mother has had to do? You must be out of your mind! Percy is going to have a smart modern pharmacy in Johannesburg and, with or without your help, I am going to ensure that he gets it with a minimum of financial burden.'

'Yes, you'll want to waste my hard earned cash on that simpering jellyfish.'

She snorted again and tightened her lips at him and the needles went clickety clack at an even faster rate. At first the relative silence was restful and Bisley was almost glad to let the worries come creeping back. Besides the problem of the oil there was now this added threat of Angus McTiver's sobriety; a great threat to his own re-election as Mayor.

Eventually the restlessness was too much for him and he stood up. 'I think I'll go for a stroll,' he said. 'Perhaps it will help me to sleep.'

He opened the door and, on his way out, looked over his shoulder and called out: 'Why don't you embroider a pink pansy on that?' He slammed the door behind him.

His home was situated in a quiet street near the river and about a mile from the centre of town. He set off slowly along the path beside the river which was flowing strongly with the January rains.

After a while he turned away from the river and down a street which led into the main thoroughfare. He continued his stroll down the main street and towards the centre of his sleeping kingdom.

He was surprised to see the ground floor of the President Hotel ablaze with lights, and as he approached he imagined he heard laughter and singing and, as he came nearer still, the clink of glasses. When he was a mere twenty yards from the bar doors he had to admit that there was a party in progress.

He hurried forward and opened the swing doors. Angus McTiver was standing on a table, his face contorted in concentration as, with amazing control, he regulated his afflatus into a surprisingly accurate rendition of 'God save the Queen'.

As the last note trailed away there was a great roar of approval and Angus dropped down from the table, grabbed a glass of amber liquid and downed it in one gulp.

With shock, Bisley looked around the room. Constable van Onselen was sprawled on a bench in a corner laughing hysterically and applauding the doctor's performance. His wet helmet rolled drunkenly on the floor beside him. The parrot was shrieking for another drink. The hotel manager and the barman had their arms around each other's shoulders and were beginning the sixth verse of *The Good Ship Venus* .

With their backs against the bar a drink-elated Lappies LeRoux and a sullen van der Watt shouted Afrikaans imprecations at each other in the course of a heated argument. They frequently raised quart bottles of beer to their lips.

Bisley stepped into the centre of the room. Someone recognised him and a shout silenced the parrot, the Venus and the argument.

'Well, it's Uncle Tom hisself. Horray for the Mayor!'

Bisley was grasped on either side and hurried up to the bar. A glassful of neat whisky was thrust into his hand and he was urged to 'drink it down, down, down' which, in his bewilderment, he did. A tankard of cold beer was then handed to him as a chaser. He grasped the tankard and steadied himself.

Over all the emotions that had rocked him, the anger, the surprise, the distress that had assailed him in the last few minutes, there was one great mitigating factor. One of Bisley's problems, the newest, dissolved in a flash. Angus was obviously back on the bottle.

With a sigh of relief, Bisley felt the whisky seep through him and, raising the tankard, he chased it to the furthest corners of his being.

Chapter 12

Amanda LeRoux quivered. So did Lappies. Their reasons for quivering were diametrically opposed to each other. Anger and fright.

Amanda's quivering two hundred and forty pounds was an awesome sight in any man's eyes. To the one hundred and fifty three pound Perpetrator of Crimes, the sight was horrific in the extreme.

Lappies crouched against the wall of the kitchen with a towel rail digging viciously but unheeded into his right kidney. His beloved wife stood, arms akimbo, next to her stove, facing her lord and master with an expression that would have daunted a pair of Rottweilers.

A pot lid clattered beside her on the stove and the contents of the pot began to spill over and fizzle. Without taking her eyes off Lappies or pausing in her diatribe for one second, she slapped the pot off the heat and on to the back of the stove. '... an' so, Mr LeRoux is so important nowadays that he can spend until three o'clock in the morning in a bar!' On the last word her voice rose to an unbelievable pitch of incredulity. A Bar, playground of the Devil. Tempter of man. Downfall of humanity.

Lappies cringed and tried to interrupt. He could have more easily stemmed the Steenrivier floods. He got no further than a parting of his lips.

'Shaddap! Pig! Loafer in bars while the family at home is forgotten. Who was to read from the Good Book after *aandete* last night? Whose children cried themselves to sleep without their father's hand on their pillows? Whose wife crept sadly into a chilly bed, alone, and asked *die Here* to protect her man?'

Lappies had to lodge a (silent) protest at this last point. Amanda never crept. Nor was her bed ever chilly. In the height of the Free State winter her enormous bulk gave off waves of thermal units that turned their lopsided bed into a furnace. For Lappies, summer meant a Turkish bath every night as he was enfolded in the grip of a centrally-heated bear and pressed mercilessly into a twin tent bosom. As these treasonous thoughts flashed through his mind he quivered anew in case she had read his thoughts.

She had to pause for breath and Lappies took a breath and exclaimed.

'But, *skat,* this was the first time in five years and it was a mistake. I did not mean ...'

Amanda had recovered her breath and she blasted him further into his towel rail with a snort of derision that would have sent a rhinoceros into permanent seclusion.

'A mistake! Who can get drunk by mistake? Who can forget a loving little wife and six beautiful children by mistake? Who can forget his God for all of nine hours every five years, all by mistake? Only LeRoux it seems. These are the mistakes that bring to an end the family and the State. These are the mistakes that drive God away from His people.'

Every 'mistake' she accentuated so that it was the lash of a whip, before which Lappies winced as if a real sjambok had swept across his face.

'Such 'mistakes' bring but shame on a man and his family. I am now the wife of a drunkard. My lovely children are those of a dissolute bar wastrel.'

Stung to the quick, Lappies shouted: 'Drunkard I am not. I tell you, for the first time in five years did I succumb to McTiver's invitation to have a small drink after the council meeting and, as van der Watt was also going, I could see no harm ...'

'No harm! No harm! Two *diakens* of the church entering a house of shame in the company of a drunken Scotsman! What are we coming to? Soon you will be mixing with *Roomse* and Jews and playing tennis on Sunday!'

The magnitude of his perfidy caused Lappies to shrink back into his towel rail. Amanda rocked like a battleship that had delivered a broadside.

'That I should live to see our home begin to crumble, our children to be without a father, my husband's love for me changed into a love of the bottle.'

With mounting horror Lappies realised she was going to wail as he saw her expression soften and her eyes begin to glisten. She continued.

'At our lovely wedding only twelve years ago, when we toasted each other with tea and promised undying love you also swore that the devil drink would never come between us ...' she sobbed her first convulsive sob ... 'and now, this is twice in only twelve years ...'

She broke down completely and, lifting her apron, began to howl uncontrollably into its red daisies and orange sunflowers. Lappies licked his dry lips apprehensively and took a tentative step towards her.

'Amanda, my *skattebol* ...' he touched her shoulder and the next second was a heap of jelly on the floor in a far corner of the room as an arm like a tree trunk smashed him away.

'Don't you touch me, you..you..you offal,' she screamed and returned to her apron. Lappies hauled himself to his feet and slunk to the doorway. He looked at his wife as she keened and wailed into her tent-like apron. He saw the gross wobbling of massive buttocks, mighty hams and gargantuan mammary appurtenances. He shook his head in bewilderment. Was it possible that this was once a dainty blossom of the veld, a mere hundred and fifty pounds of giggling love? How could anyone gain ninety pounds in twelve years? He had been about a hundred and fifty pounds for as long as he could remember. Perhaps the Turkish baths had something to do with it.

Closing the door he wandered away from the house absorbed in the mysteries of metabolism. Feeling great relief at his escape without broken bones, he headed for the security of his shop.

As he passed van der Watt's house, the front door was flung open and the big grocer stumbled out and galloped down the path followed by a torrent of abuse, a shoe, a vase complete with flowers and two glass ashtrays, one of which scored a direct hit on the back of the bullet head.

As his front door slammed, with such force that the brass door knocker fell to the ground, van der Watt leaned against his gate post and wiped his sweating forehead with a handkerchief. Gingerly he felt the back of his head and inspected his hand as if expecting to see blood.

He heard a chuckle behind him and swung around furiously. Lappies stepped back smartly and raised a placatory hand.

'Me too, Van. But yours seems worse. Last night?'

'Ja,' van der Watt said miserably, 'you would think I got drunk every day.'

'How long ago was it?'

'Three years.'

'Mine's five.'

They looked at each other in warm sympathy and walked on in silence. The tempo of their footsteps became slower and slower and stopped altogether, by some strange quirk of circumstance, immediately outside the President Bar.

Wordless, they turned sharply and entered the cool gloom behind the swing doors.

Chapter 13

Bisley shuddered and then wished that he had not. He shuddered when he thought of the previous night's drunken orgy and wished that he had not when the shudder sorely tried his aching head.

It was ten a.m. on the morning after McTiver's party and Bisley sat at the conference table awaiting his councillors. In front of him were a large bottle of aspirin, a carafe of water and his dark glasses.

The horror of the night's events arose before him. How had he allowed himself, a dignitary, to become embroiled in a common barroom thrash? In mitigation, he felt that it was the fact that his relief at seeing McTiver back on the bottle was so great that it had temporarily weakened his usually strong self-discipline.

Considering the matter overall, his present furred tongue, throbbing head and sore eyes, not to mention a liver that hung over his belt, he realised that the only bright spot in the entire kaleidoscope was the wonderful fact that Doctor McTiver had removed himself from the lists.

The presence of Lappies and van der Watt at the party was the last nail in their coffin in the Mayoral stakes: one hint to the voting populace concerning the dalliance of deacons in drinking dives would be enough.

This left only Drumpel and Gruber as possible opposition and he was sure he could successfully discredit them. Rory Morison was no problem as their pact had catered for this.

However, there was still the problem of how to whitewash his own blotted escutcheon. Agatha's performance earlier that morning had been impressive. He wished he could have been in a position to appreciate her oratory. But he had grasped some unpleasant allegations concerning his immediate ancestry.

She had performed with Boadicean majesty about family disgrace and how it would adversely affect the future of their beloved son. In vain had he protested that this had been merely an isolated incident in a life of righteousness. She had not accepted this. It was probably the beginning of worse to come. She warned him that no further misdemeanours would be tolerated. She would pack her bags and go to their son.

Even in his alcohol befuddled state Bisley had realised that, desirable as this might seem, it would certainly militate against his Mayoral chances in the future. No such scandal would be tolerated by

Palmpoppians whose sins were all hidden.

He looked at his watch and, seeing that it was ten thirty, he rose and fetched his chain of office from the cupboard and hung it around his neck. He took a few more aspirins and washed them down with a glass of water, sat down and tried to compose himself for the meeting.

As the councillors filed in, he looked carefully into the face of each one. Heinz Gruber was first. The vacant look on his face was neither reassuring nor otherwise. He always looked vacant. Lappies came next and it was with a surge of hope that Bisley noticed his hangdog look. Van der Watt looked uncomfortable and the jaw, instead of thrusting, wobbled. He tried to look conspiratorially at the Mayor but Bisley withered him with a glare.

Rory Morison came in with a look of stern disapproval and Bisley felt much the same as he had on the day, many years ago, when his mother had caught him masturbating in the bath.

Felix Drumpel's face was impassive. Bisley could read nothing from it. The undertaker probably approved of such shenanigans as they could eventually promote business for him.

Bisley's jaw dropped as Angus bounced, literally bounced, into the council chamber. The Mayor looked disbelievingly at his jaunty expression and clear eye and his greeting stabbed through Bisley's head like a hot needle.

'Top o' the mornin', Tom. Wha' aboot a heer o' th' dog?'

Bisley was routed. McTiver always came to the meetings dragging of step and jaundiced of eye. Here he was, after the orgy to end all orgies, as chipper as a fox terrier.

Bisley's expression was of such intensity that even a blind man would have had no difficulty in sensing his thoughts.

Angus chortled. 'Ginger ale, Tom. Th' aunly drrink as cleen as the' Hielan' due. Na murre fer me the amber de'il.'

Bisley glugged and gargled something unintelligible and tried to pull himself together. He felt that, had he not been sitting down, he would have fallen. His knees had that watery feeling one gets during a brake failure. With an effort he pulled himself together and faced the meeting.

'I regret, gentlemen, that I can report no progress of substance. Beyond instilling the idea of patriotism into Labuschagne's mind, which I have done, I can think of no way in which to persuade him.' He felt that right now he would have traded all the oil in the world for one good hangover remedy.

'Then why don't you drop the whole thing,' grumbled van der Watt, 'and let us all live in peace.'

'Mister van der Watt,' snarled Morison, 'it seems that you lack the slightest tinge of vision. Why don't you resign from this council and go and live in selfish peace. Let the men get on with men's work.'

Van der Watt yelled at Morison: 'The Devil quotes scripture for his own ends! You do not fool me with your talk of self-sacrifice. You are not interested in Palmpoppiesfontein. You care only for yourself. You have shown your true colours only too clearly over the last few years. I am ashamed to admit that I have been party to some of your swindles.'

'Careful, *ou maat*,' warned Lappies, 'he is a blerry lawyer. He'll twish everything you say.' Lappies ended with a loud belch.

Bisley sniffed, and sniffed again.

'Beer?' he said. 'Do I smell beer?' He looked closely at Lappies. 'You've been drinking.'

'Sho what?'

'How dare you come to a council meeting under the influence?'

'He's not,' shouted van der Watt. 'We just had a few beers together.'

'My God! You too! What's happening to this council? Just a crowd of drunks!'

'Follow m' leader, Tom,' cackled Angus.

'You shut up, you drunken reprobate.'

'Bloody nerve!'

'Damn drunkard, calling me a swindler!'

'Deacons of the church, drunk before noon!'

'Bloody slimy bastard, McTiver, getting us all drunk while you drink ginger-ale.'

The meeting dissolved into a clamour of accusations and epithets. They were approaching blows when Drumpel, the only one who had remained calm, stood up and silenced them all with a great shout:

'WHAT ABOUT THE BLOODY OIL?'

The silence continued for a while as rapid breathing quietened and the gentlemen composed themselves, darting looks of shame at each other.

Morison cast his evil eye at them. 'Unless we are prepared to forget our differences and attack this problem as a team, we may as well all resign right now.'

'Quite, quite,' agreed Bisley pompously.

'Well, why doesn't the Mayor give us something constructive to work on,' said LeRoux querulously, 'instead of all this rubbish about where to build the hospital and the fire station, and asking us to select a good site for the statue ...'

'Statue!' He was cut off by the simultaneous gasp from the others.

'Yes, a statue. Didn't he speak to you all about it?'

'A statue of whom?' they chorused.

There was another silence, an uncomfortable silence. Slowly all eyes turned to focus on Bisley. He made a few ineffectual passes with his hands and his attempt at a light-hearted smile was a sickly grin.

Morison realised that he had yet again to gallop to the rescue.

'Gentlemen, I feel that this is the time for me, once and for all, to calm your fears and silence your doubts. I was hoping not to have to use this weapon or even to make it known. I see that I must now take you into my confidence. This must go no further. At this stage we may not have to use my secret weapon. We still await a final decision from Labuschagne. Then, if necessary I shall force Labuschagne to come to terms.'

'How?' It was a chant. An explosive syllable filled with excitement and beer fumes. They were like kids awaiting the answer to a riddle, or for the magician to pull a rabbit from his hat.

Slowly, Morison selected a cigarette from his gold case, tapped the end, and lit it. Lappies was quivering again. Not with fright this time. He resembled a daschund that had cornered a mouse and was waiting for the word to attack.

Van der Watt was blinking rapidly. Things were moving a bit too fast for him and he wondered how poor old Heinz was doing. A quick look told him that he wasn't OK. His mouth hung open and his eyes were glazed. Drumpel and McTiver remained impassive, but rats were gnawing at their vitals.

'Gentlemen,' Morison continued, 'Sarel Labuschagne will have a choice. He will either voluntarily sell his mining rights or, if he wishes, the whole farm, or else he will be forced to part with the oil. Obviously, if he does so voluntarily it will be on his own terms and at his price and there will be no harm done. If he remains adamant against exploitation of the find, I shall force him legally to abandon all his rights to the oil.'

'B..b..but, Rory,' stammered Bisley, 'how can you?'

Relief was starting to overwhelm him. When it did his knees would buckle and his muscles liquefy. But, despite his great faith in Morison he could not yet abandon himself to the narcosis of uninhibited relief.

Morison opened his briefcase and extracted a document.

'This is an extract from the files of the Provincial Deeds Office,' He held it up and proceeded to read.

'The undernoted areas will be subject to the provisions of Section l, Paragraph A (ii) of the Ordinance of the Orange Free State.' He skipped over a few names and references and then continued, ... 'the magisterial districts of Koffiefontein and Palmpoppiesfontein including the rural areas thereof where not classified as commonage and notwithstanding the provisions of the Farmers' Assistance Act of 1952 as amended ...'

He trailed off and replaced the document. The faces around him were still blank and he realised that he might as well have been reading Greek to them.

'Section l, Paragraph A (ii) of the Ordinance,' he continued patiently, 'is concerned with the rights of landowners as regards the content of the land other than its productivity. It is known as the Mining Rights Exclusion and means, in essence, that no one discovering minerals on his land has the automatic right to mine them. They are the prior property of the relevant magistrate of the Borough Council, of course representing the State, and may be either taken over by the local authority or a clearance given to the landowner to develop the find. In this case we will obviously tell Sarel that he either applies for a clearance and gets on with exploiting the oil or he is kicked off his farm.'

There was a gasp of admiration from the assembly. They sat back in their chairs and beamed expansively at their golden boy. Bisley tried to get up to shake Morison's hand, but his knees refused to function. From the depths of a throat dried by tension and in a voice trembling with emotion, Bisley said:

'Gentlemen, we owe a debt of gratitude to Mr Morison that cannot be measured, let alone paid. I ask you for a unanimous vote of thanks to our dedicated and brilliant legal man. I ask you to ensure that in due course the town realises the depth of its indebtedness to this fearless crusader. I trust that in the exciting days that lie ahead you ...'

He was interrupted rudely by McTiver who said, 'Why no' put a statchoo o' Rory in th' market square, thin?'

Bisley collapsed and the others sniggered, but Angus jumped to his feet and said: 'I'll tell yer wun thing, gen'lmen, I doan like this. No' a wee bittie. 'Tis a foul way o' winnin' an' I'll hae no part o' it.' He stamped out, slamming the door. Bisley shrugged and raised his eyebrows. The councillors sat tight.

'We must not let personal feelings stand in the way of our country's good. Correct?'

'Correct,' they echoed in unison and filed out, leaving Bisley and Morison in close conversation.

Bisley felt that it was unnecessary to wait any longer for old Sarel to make up his mind or for any results to be forthcoming from the Mortimer/Tina front. They decided to move at once and that Morison would throw down the gauntlet to Sarel in the form of a registered letter acquainting the farmer with the legal position.

Chapter 14

Old Kleinbooi accepted the tobacco and carefully filled his pipe before handing the pouch back to Sarel. They lit up and puffed in contented silence for a while. The two men sat on a log in the shade of a bluegum tree near the river. The sheep were being driven down from the early slopes and were fording the river across a concrete causeway. The experienced eyes of the farmer and the headman watched for any signs of injury or unusual features in the flock.

Kleinbooi was over seventy-five years old. His black eyes, framed in his weather-beaten face, flickered over the sheep, missing nothing.

'The grass is good this year,' said Sarel.

'As in many years. The Lord smiles on the baas yet again.'

'And in the droughts? Why has the Lord not smiled on me then?'

'The baas has been out of the Lord's sight in those years. The baas must have done ill.'

'Ag, Kleinbooi, when have I done evil?'

'Only the baas and the Lord know, my baas.'

Sarel chewed his pipe stem and thought carefully. Perhaps the old devil was right. But some of the droughts had been very severe. Surely he hadn't been that bad?

How was he to regard this latest trial, certainly the worst of his life. Droughts eventually broke and the farm came to life once more. Storms and floods left their mark, but those were eventually covered by time. Disease could kill off all the sheep, but there were always more sheep to walk the camps of Boomplaas. The crops could fail one year, but grow to ten feet the next. No, all the problems of the past had been unable to wrest Boomplaas away from him.

This was the end. If he could accept the opinion of others as to where his duty lay, it would seem that where the wrath of God, the elements and nature had tried and failed, the internal combustion engine would succeed.

'The baas is sad. How can his heart be heavy when the sheep are so well before his eyes and the mielies are eight feet high behind him?'

'Ou Kleinbooi, I am more than sad. This may be the last time that you and I can sit here and count our sheep.'

'Baas, I know I am old, but there is no reason for me to die for yet a few seasons.'

'You conceited old bastard,' Sarel laughed, 'I'm not thinking of your death. I'm not even thinking of my own, although,' he suddenly felt heavy, as if death had indeed touched him, 'although if what troubles me does happen, I am sure that my death will soon follow.'

'Of what does the baas speak?'

'I may have to sell the farm, Kleinbooi, soon.'

'*Magtig*, the baas must not speak so. And if the baas is short of money, ou Kleinbooi can help.'

Interested in this side issue, Sarel said, 'And where do you have any money?'

'Baas, I have never had need of money since the day I came as an *umfaan* to work for your father. All my needs have been met. Most of my pay is in the Post Office. I can give the Baas six thousand rand to help.'

'You are a kind old *skelm*, Kleinbooi. But money is not the cause of my care. No, I fear that the farm will have to be given over to the oil.'

'Oil? Oil, my baas. What is this?'

Sarel proceeded to tell Kleinbooi about all the events of the past few weeks and his own heartache at the avarice of the townspeople, who somehow seemed to have right on their side. When he had finished speaking the old black man shook his head in wonder.

'Baas, if the farms are taken for this oil, then where do the sheep and the mielies come from to clothe and feed the people who are going to use the oil?'

'Not all the farms, Kleinbooi. Just Boomplaas.'

'But Boomplaas is a queen among farms. Why can they not look elsewhere?'

'I don't know. They say oil is so scarce in our country that they must take it wherever they can find it.'

'So what will the baas do?'

'I will take all this oil money for which I have no need, and I will go to live in a city and sit on the stoep drinking coffee until I die.'

'Kleinbooi will die without waiting for the coffee!'

'No, Kleinbooi, I will give you land at another farm, with my son Petrus, in the Transvaal.'

'Will baas be there too?'

'No.'

'Then I do not want the land.'

'Ah, old friend, you add to my cares.'

'Fear not, baas, Kleinbooi will die with Boomplaas. But why cut out his heart so that others may feed even better than they do?'

'They say it is to serve my country, which needs what lies under my lands.'

'Baas has served his country enough. To turn Vlakte into Boomplaas is enough service for one life span and to that the baas has added many sons who serve the land as he did.'

'Enough is a word unknown in the world of money, ou Kleinbooi.'

Silence fell again as they sucked at their pipes; a silence broken only by the splashing of the sheep through the ford and their occasional bleat. Then they heard the deep voices of the approaching drovers – voices which complemented the silence and did not shatter it.

After the last sheep had passed, followed by some of Kleinbooi's grandsons, Sarel and the old servant followed them. Kleinbooi turned off towards his kraal without another word, but not before Sarel had seen tears in his eyes.

As Sarel neared his home, the sun slid down behind the mountains. He saw a trail of dust from the main road and remembered that Tina and Williams Mortimer were coming to supper.

Chapter 15

Morison waddled through Tina's reception office and settled himself at his desk, leaving the connecting door open.

'Tina,' he called, 'please bring your notebook, there's an urgent letter to get off.'

Tina sharpened her pencil and went through, settling herself on the opposite side of his desk. Since Willem had told her about his meeting with Morison and the slimy lawyer's suggestion, she was not feeling as loyal to her employer as she had before.

Expressionless, Morison dictated: 'To Mr S G Labuschagne, P O Box 48, Palmpoppiesfontein.'

Tina looked up in surprise and Morison, seeing her hesitation said: 'I'm afraid this is not a pleasant task for either of us, my dear, but, when you have written the letter, you will understand that it has to be done.'

'In brief, your grandfather is to be forced, legally, to either sell his farm or to grant rights to an approved prospecting company. You could do much to assist both your grandfather and us..er..um..the town, by impressing on Sarel the facts surrounding the position.'

'Forced to sell? Mr Morison how can anyone be forced to sell anything?'

'I'm afraid, my dear, that in their wisdom our government and provincial authorities have catered for such items of national importance such as gold, oil and various other items, to prevent their being either exploited in the wrong way, monopolistically for instance, or not being developed at all, to the detriment of the economy. I will quote in this letter the relevant Act which forces your grandfather to come to terms.'

When she had taken down the notes, Tina left Morison's office with a look of distaste on her face and went back to her typewriter where she banged out the offensive letter, hating the way in which she was being forced to aid in the crucifixion of her beloved old grandfather.

Before she took the letter in for signature she checked the sickening phrases quickly.

'... it is with extreme regret that we have to take this step but must assure you that it is purely the result of your own inability to recognise what the council feels is the indisputable duty of anyone in your position. This notwithstanding, the decision to enforce the ordinance was not taken lightly and only after lengthy deliberation on the part of our respected Mayor and his council.

'The decision was unanimous and calls for your reply within seven days. Should you apply for the necessary clearance to develop the natural resources of Boomplaas, permission will be given immediately. In the same measure, immediate action will be taken to enforce the ordinance at the expiry of the seven days of grace.'

When Tina dropped the original of the letter on Morison's desk her face was white with rage. After signing the letter Morison said, 'Tina, I do hope that you can see our point of view and I would suggest that you try to be with Sarel when he receives this letter. I would like to deliver it and explain, but it must go by registered post.'

'I'm sure you would like to deliver it, Mr Morison; just as I would like to deliver a foreclosure on your home's mortgage, but I suppose you've been in local politics long enough to have eliminated all such financial burdens.'

'Tina! I don't understand your attitude. I'm only doing my job!'

'And I've never seen anyone quite so much in love with his work!'

Tina stalked out and slammed the door. She sat herself down at her typewriter and wrote a letter of resignation and, leaving it in the machine, collected her belongings, plus a copy of the letter she had had to write to Sarel, and left the office for the last time.

'But Willem, how can a law be so unjust?' Tina was close to tears.

'There are many unjust laws, Tina, but there are others which seem unjust until you look into the reasoning behind them.' Spuds was trying to talk himself out of exploding into anger just as much as he was trying to calm Tina.

'But to force a man to give up his home, a place that has been the home of his grandparents before: surely this can never be right. It's not as if he has done anything wrong. He's turned Boomplaas into something of which the whole district is proud. He's always paid his taxes and made contributions to every worthy cause – even some doubtful ones. Do you know he even gave R500 to that new Roman Catholic convent in Koffiefontein?'

'Under normal circumstances, Tina, I would feel that this need not be as unpleasant as it appears. With careful handling, there may be no need to wreck Boomplaas. As far as this section of the ordinance is concerned, it is quite reasonable so that strategic minerals can be exploited to the greatest good of the State and the community in general.

'However, I am not trying to defend the actions of Bisley and his gang. Unfortunately it seems that they have the law on their side, but the whole thing could have been handled with more tact, and not in such a hurry. *Oom* Sarel has not been given a decent chance to think about this and consider what it would mean. I think that he would be reasonable in his own time but this letter and threats will make him even more stubborn. Bisley and Co. can't wait to dip their dirty paws into the oil.'

'I hope there will be some way in which *Oupa* can make sure that they get nothing.' Tina sniffed and patted her nose with a tissue.

Spuds drove slowly towards the farm in the golden twilight. To Tina everything looked even more beautiful than usual. But her heart felt heavy when she realised just how much heavier her grandfather's spirits would be.

As they stopped outside the house Tina pointed to a graceful plane tree near the tennis court.

'That is the tree that *Oupa* planted when I was born, nearly twenty years ago.'

'He planted trees for every birth, didn't he?'

'Yes, with the names on them of each child and grandchild.'

They went into the house. *Tante* Bessie was, as usual, in the kitchen. Sarel was also there, making a nuisance of himself. When they entered he came forward and gripped their arms.

'Ha! There you are. Now we can have a drink. I think I needs *maar* a few drinks today.'

Spuds thought Sarel didn't yet realise just how correct he was. He thought that the old man's lightheartedness was a bit forced and the expression on Tina's face told him that he was right.

Sarel poured brandies for Spuds and himself – they looked like treble tots – and threw in the usual teaspoon of water. He gave Tina a glass of muscadel and they toasted each other and drank. As usual Sarel came to the point without any bush beating.

'I have decided to let them have their blerry oil.'

He looked quickly at Tina and Spuds as their breath gushed out simultaneously.

'*Wat makeer julle?*'

'Nothing, *Oom.* Brandy's a bit strong; went down the wrong way.'

'Yes, so did this strong wine,' said Tina with a nervous giggle.'

'*Kaf!* Rubbish,' snorted Sarel. 'You've drunk muscadel since you were six years old!'

The two young people looked uncomfortable and Sarel looked at them suspiciously. Tina felt as if the copy of the letter in her bag would burst into flames at any moment.

'Yes, I have decided that I must be wrong. Mind you, I can't agree that anyone should have to pay such a price at the end of a life of hard work.

'I remember that my old father told me that responsibility makes a man. I have accepted my life and its many obligations and I think I have been a man. Now, if I throw away what appears to be my greatest responsibility, then I will die knowing that I have failed my last trial. What hurts is that these vultures,' his voice was contemptuous, 'these *aasvoëls* at the Town Hall will grow fat on my sacrifice. You can be quite sure that they will have their hands in the scrum that is to follow.'

'Oh, *Oupa*,' sobbed Tina and rushed into her grandfather's arms. 'You can't give Boomplaas away!'

Sarel looked at Spuds over Tina's golden head and lifted his bushy eyebrows quizzically. He shrugged.

'But you thought that I should?'

Tina sobbed even louder and Spuds shrugged back at Sarel. Tina jumped up and ran into the kitchen where *Tante* Bessie could be heard comforting her.

'*Oom* Sarel,' said Spuds, 'I feel dirty. I know I have tried to influence you to release this oil, but I don't think I realised then, or will I ever quite understand, just what all this means to you.'

'Ag, never to worry my boy. Old people are often selfish. Why must I sit on top of all this prosperity, not taking it for myself because I don't need it, and not allowing others, who do need it, to benefit?'

'Including Bisley and Co.?'

'The bastards!'

'Sarel,' Bessie called from the kitchen, 'please come here for a minute.'

Sarel shambled out and Tina came in, suspiciously dry-eyed. She sat down quickly next to Spuds and asked quietly:

'What can we do about the letter? It's no good upsetting him now.'

'We must not show him that copy, but how can we stop the registered one arriving tomorrow?'

'I know,' said Tina. 'I usually collect the mail for him. I'll sign for it and then tear it up. You must go to the councillors and tell them never to mention to anyone how they had tried to use force on Oupa. He must never know about the letter.'

'Right. The next thing will be to help him to go about this business in the right way. I still think it might be unnecessary to ruin the farm.'

Sarel and Bessie came in and Tina changed the subject. Sarel charged their glasses.

'Dinner is nearly ready,' said Bessie.

'What do you think of *Oom* Sarel's decision, *Tante*,' asked Spuds.

'My husband gave me this home and, through the years, by his hard work, he has made me a very happy and comfortable woman. To do this he has taken on all our responsibilities himself. His decisions have always been correct. How can I now disagree? How can I complain after more than forty years of comfort if my way of life must change? I still know that Sarel will always do what is right. It will hurt me grievously to see this farm destroyed; it will hurt me more to see my man destroyed by shame.'

Tina looked at her grandmother with pride. Sarel took her hand and patted it. Spuds felt even more dirty.

The silence persisted for a while as the level of their drinks was lowered. Suddenly the ubiquitous dogs jumped up from under chairs and tables and ran, barking madly, to the open door and out into the night. Eventually, over the din, they heard the sound of a car approaching. Sarel shouted at the dogs and their frenzied barking subsided into an occasional yap as the car slid to a halt in the drive.

Sarel headed for the door but their visitor beat them to it. McTiver marched into the room and planted himself firmly in the middle of the carpet looking around pugnaciously.

'Sarel, I've come ter tell ye. I'll hae no parrrt o' it. Tis a dirrty idee o' a dirrtier mind.'

Sarel and Bessie looked puzzled. Tina and Spuds squirmed with apprehension.

'No part of what dirty idea, Angus?' asked Sarel.

'Tha' letter aboot th' ordinance, forcin' ye tae shell th' farrm an' th' oil.'

'What!' Sarel exploded, spilling brandy over a nearby dog.

Tina and Spuds looked at each other. 'Stout Cortes on his Darien Peak' held no more wild surmise.

Tina realised that between them Sarel and Angus were to get hopelessly confused.

'*Oupa*,' she said, 'it appears that there is some law which says that if you have gold or oil or something rare and precious in your land you have to allow it to be mined.' She took a copy of the letter from her bag and gave it to Sarel. 'The original of that is in the post to you.'

Slowly and in silence, Sarel read it, mouthing each word soundlessly. The atmosphere in the room was that of the veld before a great storm, when the silence becomes tangible and birds hurry overhead to shelter.

The dogs shrank away from Sarel and dipped their tails as they scurried off into the night. The occupants of the room found their fingernails biting into their palms.

Sarel looked up, crumpling the paper. His jaw was set tight but his eyes glistened.

'*Varke*,' he breathed, '*onnosele varke. Onnosele gulsige varke.* Now they will not touch one square inch of my land, if I have to spend my last cent fighting them right to the Union Buildings.'

'Atta boy, Sarel. Tha's th' way. Fix th' bassards. Shorry Tina, Bessie. Shtill they're bassards.'

Spuds looked closely at the little doctor who noticed his glance. 'Yesh,' he said gleefully. 'I've ha' a few drams, an muure te come. I shtopped thinkin' I'd hae a crack at bein' th' mayor. I'd rather be a drunk than mayor o' tha' lousy burg an' mixed up wi' they bums. Back tae th' ol' bo'l fer me an' happy I'll be. Hic.'

They sat down and Sarel poured even larger tots than before, including Angus in the round. Suddenly the rage which had been boiling in Sarel exploded and he flung his glass at the wall and jumped to his feet in a torrent of imprecations and fist shaking. The gist of it was that Bisley and Co. had been issued by the miscegenation of a skunk and a warthog and would shortly be destined to live out what remained of their lives in emasculation.

Sarel stormed out of the room and Bessie followed him. Angus grabbed the bottle and after filling his glass, told Tina and Spuds of the goings-on in the council. He seemed intent on finishing the bottle so Spuds and Tina decided to leave.

It was a thoughtful Spuds who drove Tina home and deposited her outside her aunt's house. Absently, he drove away without even kissing her goodnight and she cried herself to sleep but more because her dear old grandfather was sad.

Chapter 16

In the days that followed, Sarel stalked about his farm muttering and yelling his anger at whoever or whatever blotted his horizon. The healing tissues of his bum throbbed in pain as his high-pressured blood pulsed through them. The pain reminded him of the beginnings of the situation, the ignominy of his predicament, and hardened his already granite-like hatred of those he now classed as enemies.

The usually vacant eyes of his sheep now seemed to look at him with soft and trusting brown orbs of total dependence. The mielies, waved by the wind, rustled their foliage to sound like a sibilant 'please' as he stamped around his fields.

In his imagination he saw his groves of oak and tambotie trees replaced by blackened steel structures. And he swore. He swore terribly and expressively. But even this did not help. Inside him the conflict grew more and more unbearable. That which he had so recently accepted as a duty became the imposition of a ruthless dictator. The thought of his sacrifice being offered on the altar of Bisley's current account at the bank, made his rage a red mist in which the faces of his tormentors laughed at him out of the branches of his bluegum trees.

Kleinbooi and the other farm staff avoided him and quietly got on with the business of running the farm.

Bessie sweated like a galley-slave in the kitchen preparing dish after dish of exotica to try to tempt Sarel out of his mood of orbital fury.

Tina and Spuds stayed away, nervously awaiting developments.

The atmosphere in the council chamber was relaxed, even jolly. There was no bickering. They held a short meeting each day to congratulate themselves in general and Rory Morison in particular. They planned plans and schemed schemes. They devoted one happy meeting to inducting Hannes Duvenage, a local farmer who, having property in town, was eligible for council duty. He was to replace Angus who had handed in his letter of resignation accompanied by a verbal elucidation of its content in a torrent of whisky-laden language which had not bothered them at all.

But Rory Morison became increasingly morose as the days of grace allowed to Sarel elapsed without result; without communication of any kind from Boomplaas. His quietness went unnoticed until the fifth day when a particularly light-hearted meeting had culminated in a series of excellent jokes through which Morison sat in silence. Noticing that his ally was not even smiling at Hannes Duvenage's last excruciatingly funny story, Bisley asked him what was wrong.

'Nothing, Tom, nothing really, but I would like to know which way the cat is going to jump.'

Good old Rory, thought Bisley. Always so diligent. So concerned. So dependable.

The car sped along the newly-tarred road between Palmpoppiesfontein and Koffiefontein. Tina and Spuds sat in silence. Both were frowning. Spuds' frown was one of intense concentration, Tina's one of sheer puzzlement.

'But why must we go to Koffiefontein?'

'Because I want to look up the ordinance.'

'But there's a copy at the magistrate's office at Palmpops.'

'I don't want to be seen. I've an idea that there is something fishy.'

'Like what?'

'Wait and see.'

So Tina had to be content to sit in silence while they drove. Then she had to sit in a café and drink lime juice until it was coming out of her ears while Spuds spent about an hour in the courthouse, closeted with the clerk of the court and copies of the Ordinance of the Orange Free State and the Constitution of the Republic of South Africa.

When he came back to her he was wearing a smile that made her heart leap.

'Now let's go and have a real drink,' he said, 'and then some lunch.'

'But tell me. What have you done?'

'Sshh, my love, later.'

So Tina had to contain herself and drink more lime juice, this time with gin added, and plough through a mixed grill that under different circumstances she would have enjoyed. Throughout the meal Spuds wore his infuriating smile and spoke of trivialities until Tina felt she would scream.

Then they drove home at a leisurely pace while Spuds gave Tina an account of his rugby days and his cricket days and his water polo prowess and generally chattered on until Tina's frustration matched that of her grandfather stomping around his farm in exasperation.

After depositing a protesting Tina at her aunt's house, Spuds drove around to the offices of Dickson and Lee and spent some time with the competent little man who 'did the books' of Boomplaas.

When he emerged and drove away his smile was broader still.

It was with some difficulty that Sarel was persuaded to sit still for a few minutes and to keep quiet. It was the evening of the sixth day of the ultimatum and the atmosphere at Boomplaas was one of despair. Sarel had accepted that there was no hope for him against the law. He also knew that his stubbornness and pride would never permit capitulation. The outcome of irresistible force meeting immovable object was going to be a very dirty business.

The Voortrekker blood of his grandfather and the commando blood of his father ran strongly in Sarel's veins. And he nursed his hate and his pride. This was his fight. It must have been the same for his forefathers who had retreated from valley to koppie to mountains, never admitting defeat although knowing it to be inevitable; never allowing despair, although knowing their cause was hopeless.

He was annoyed to see a smile on Williams Mortimer's face. After all, he was just another damned *Engelse* and probably glad to see a *boer* deprived by his own government of something overlooked by the English invaders of the past.

He was more hurt than angry to see that Tina seemed unconcerned. Could one expect a love of the land in youth today? The call of the big city was strong. Yes, blast it, one should be entitled to look for good solid farm blood in a line such as the Labuschagne/Van Lingen marriage. Even in the girls.

The inner conflict showed clearly on his expressive face. Spuds, Tina and Bessie were in the sitting-room with him, waiting for him to simmer down. It was only *Tante* Bessie's intervention that had coaxed Sarel away from his self-imposed isolation to come and listen to what that damned oil man had to say.

He was very surprised at Spuds' first question.

'*Oom* Sarel, how many tons per hectare, on the average, have you reaped for the last five years?'

'You are trying to make the blow even more painful young man. These last five years have been among the best.'

'How many tons, Mr Labuschagne?'

Sarel noted the 'Mr' and the sterner tone of voice. He backed down a little and answered quietly. 'About four tons, I suppose.'

'Five and a half tons, to be exact. And how much for your wool?'

'B..b..but how do you know,' stammered Sarel.

'How much per pound, Mr Labuschagne?' Again the stern tone of voice got through.

'About eighty-five cents,' he said almost meekly.

'In fact, your average price has been one hundred and five cents per pound,' Spuds told him.

'But, how do you know all this and, anyway,' getting impatient and angry again, 'what's all this got to do with this oil trouble?'

Spuds took a piece of paper out of his pocket and gave it to Sarel who adjusted his spectacles and read quietly. Then he said, 'I don't understand this. What is it?'

'It is an extract from the appendix to the State Ordinance under the section on agriculture. It supersedes and modifies where necessary all Provincial Ordinances.'

'But all it says is that High Yield farms are exempt from the provisions of local ordinance and fall under the direct representational office of the Minister of Agriculture ...' He trailed off. 'An' so?'

Spuds handed him another piece of paper which he took and read carefully. 'A High Yield farm is one producing at the following rates or higher..mumble..mumble..wool, ninety-five cents per pound..maize, four tons per hectare. So Boomplaas is a High Yield farm!'

'That's right, which means that the only person who can even permit mining here is the Minister himself, or his office.'

The excitement that ensued caused the dogs to erupt in a frenzy of barking, while everyone was shouting and kissing and laughing hysterically. Gradually they quietened down and Sarel became serious again. 'Man,' he said, 'this is *lekker.* Now old Bisley and his gang will get the dirty end of the stick. But it still doesn't mean that I won't have to give up Boomplaas. If the oil is needed then it must be taken. That I have decided, so I suppose Bisley will win anyway.' The smile of triumph had quickly faded from Sarel's face. His pleasure had been short lived.

'No, I have an idea, *Oom* Sarel. Listen.'

He outlined his plan at the end of which they were all smiling again. Sad smiles, but those from which much of the sting had been removed.

Chapter 17

Morison climbed wearily out of his car, crossed the pavement and mounted the stairs to the council chambers. The Town Hall clock, banging out the hour of ten o'clock, sounded like the knell of doom to him.

For one of the few times in his life, it seemed that he had gambled and lost. If there was no reply from Sarel today, all was lost. Failure to produce the oil and its prosperity would not be tolerated by the populace; Morison's failure would not be tolerated by Bisley; and Bisley's collapse would scatter the council. In short, all hell would break loose.

So far, Morison had been able to keep his gamble to himself, it being accepted on its face value by the councillors *en bloc*, but if Sarel called his bluff, then Morison would be forced to reveal to the council his own inadequacy – his failure. One did not act independently of the council. He had.

He hesitated on the threshold of the room. They were all there, already seated around the council table. They looked stern. Morison realised that his imagination was running away with him. He pulled himself together as Bisley snapped at him.

'Come on Rory, we can't wait all day!'

Morison took his place and for the first time saw an envelope on the table in front of the Mayor. A cold hand clutched his heart.

'Well, gentlemen,' said Bisley importantly, 'here we have a letter, delivered by special messenger, from Sarel Labuschagne. I feel that it would not be presumptuous to say that it contains his application for clearance to exploit the oil fields of Boomplaas.

'I hope it is. It would be much better if he retained ownership of his land and developed the oil commercially. In this scenario we would have a lot more..er..control over his activities and our in..er, our town's interests.'

'If he elects to sell out completely and a remote prospecting company moves in, things will be more difficult for us. However, if ...'

He was, as usual, interrupted by van der Watt.

'Man, Bisley, why must you go on and on. Open the bloody envelope and tell us what he says. Then if there's anything to discuss, we'll all have a chance to say something.'

Bisley glared at him tight-lipped, and muttered something about ignorant polony-slicing Dutchmen with no soul and no feeling for the great dramatic events of life.

He resolutely slit open the envelope and extracted a sheet of typewritten paper. He read it with a puzzled frown on his face.

'Well then, get on with it!' chanted the councillors in exasperation.

'It's an invitation,' said Bisley in a mystified tone of voice.

'Invitation? To what?'

'A *braaivleis!*'

'Oh, for God's sake!' Morison could stand no more tension. His ulcer was bleeping like a sputnik. He grabbed the letter and began to read.

'Dear Mr Mayor and esteemed councillors of Palmpoppiesfontein, I am in receipt of your letter of the 16th instant. I regret the delay in sending my reply but, as you will appreciate, the decision has not been an easy one.

'Firstly, let me applaud your loyalty to your duty and your single-minded approach to the matter for the good of the community. I know that your decision to enforce the ordinance must have cost a great deal of soul-searching and that, if any of you worthy gentlemen had been involved in the position in which I now am, your decision to apply the law would have been the same.

'I would ask you to allow me an extension of the period of grace to next Saturday, the 28th. Naturally I appreciate your position and will comply with the provisions of all relevant laws, but I feel that this is a matter of grave moment and historic in the annals of our district. I therefore propose to make a public announcement of my intentions at my farm, Boomplaas, on the abovementioned date.

'The function will be a monster *braaivleis* to which I have already invited two hundred people whom I feel to be fully representative of the town and district.

'You, Mr Mayor, and your councillors and your ladies I would like to be the principal guests. I intend to make much of your part in the current developments and to commend you to the acclaim of the townspeople who have great regard for your competence.

'I am presuming your acceptance and approval and am proceeding with my plans accordingly.

Yours very sincerely,

Sarel Labuschagne.'

Morison stopped reading and the worried frown did not leave his face.

'This is not Sarel,' he said. 'He couldn't write like that in a hundred years.'

'What does it matter who wrote it? He signed it and it seems a jolly good idea to me,' said Bisley in excitement. 'I think we should formally accede to his request for an extension and accept the invitation.'

'Do you think there will be *sosaties?*' asked Heinz Gruber plaintively.
'Eh?' snapped Bisley.
'*Sosaties.* I can't bear a *braai* without *sosaties.*'
'Gruber, you are going, *sosaties* or not.'
Morison still looked worried. 'He still doesn't say what he intends to do,' he complained.
'He's capitulated. That's all we need to know. Good old Sarel, he's going to give us a public pat on the back as well. I know I got through to him along the lines of duty and patriotism.'
'I still don't see why he couldn't have sent in his application for a clearance or decision to sell the farm. He could still have had the pleasure of his big-hearted announcement on Saturday.'
'Oh, don't be such an old woman, Rory. You've done a grand job on this. Now relax and let's plan our strategy from next week onwards.'
'Yes, let's get back to thinking about a new name,' said Lappies.
'You know,' said van der Watt, looking pensive like a newly castrated bull, 'I think this has all been very hard on ou Sarel and I think we should perhaps ask him to choose a new name for the town. It's the least we can do for him, to give him a feeling of importance. After all, what's in a name? Even if he thinks it should remain as it is, let's give him the right to decide. Old Felix is right. The oil and the money will do their stuff. No one will care about the name.'
Looking a bit sick, Bisley hummed and hawed and said that it was perhaps a very charitable idea but what if the old coot insisted on a name even worse than their present one? He went on to suggest that perhaps he, Bisley, should go out to the farm and prime the old chap with a couple of names and let him propose one during his Saturday announcement as if it was his own idea. At least the council could ensure an acceptable name.
'An' what guarantee have we that you will recommend to him the name we decide on?' growled Drumpel with an unexpected show of ferocity. Felix had, over the last couple of weeks, been slowly working himself up to a pitch of justifiable anger at what he saw as Bisley's inexorable climb to the top of this particular dung heap. But, if ever there was a solid dependable type whose emotions were under control and who would therefore be able to administer a city with impartiality, surely it was to be found in the person of the undertaker?
'Really, Mr Drumpel!' Bisley exclaimed in shock. 'I do hope you are not suggesting that ...'
Again he was interrupted, by the grocer, the draper and the undertaker in unison.
'We are suggesting just that, Mr Mayor. Sarel sees us all.'
'Well! I've never been so insulted,' blustered Bisley, but his brain was

working at 3000 revs per minute.

The meeting came to an abrupt end. The atmosphere was not conducive to further discussion. The councillors filed out in silence.

The road between Palmpoppiesfontein and Boomplaas saw some heavy traffic that afternoon. By evening Sarel had had a succession of visitors and when the last one had departed he exploded into a paroxysm of laughter in which he was joined by all the dogs. The din was so intense that old Kleinbooi came running with a *knobkerrie.*

When Sarel told him the whole story they started off all over again, Sarel's roar and the dogs' barking highlighted by the descant of the old black gentleman's high-pitched cackle.

'And on Saturday and Sunday you and your people must feast, ou Kleinbooi,' said Sarel. '*Slag* six sheep for yourselves and brew much beer. Boomplaas must ring to your festivities and ours.'

In the days preceding the *braaivleis* a series of visitors called at Boomplaas and the first to arrive was a smiling, hand-washing Thomas Bisley. In his conversation he dropped ingratiating hints about solidarity with Sarel in the golden years that lay ahead and said how honoured he would be if the feelings of his council concerning the birth of 'Bisleyburg' were reflected by Sarel.

Ou Sarel had also mentioned, just in passing, that, while he would not like to be thought of as taking too much advantage of his gift to the community, he would certainly make urgent representations to the electorate concerning the re-election to office of the present incumbent.

Bisley's joy was complete and he drove home in a haze of non-alcoholic intoxication. He pranced into the house and amazed his lizard-faced wife by kissing her soundly and sending her off to the ladies' outfitters to order a selection of dresses more befitting the high station to which they would ascend. The town would bear his name – the name of the re-elected mayor!

Sarel's next visitor had been an unintelligible Heinz Gruber who had mumbled something about free services to all the farm vehicles when he became mayor; of course that was as long as Sarel didn't mind the work being done by mechanics as he himself would be too busy with the affairs of local government.

Sarel had given him assurances similar to those he'd given Bisley, mentioning such possibilities as 'Grubersdorp' and how elegant Heinz would look with a chain around his neck.

Mrs Gruber also found herself packed off to the dress shop.

The visit by Lappies LeRoux was straightforward and was nothing but an exhortation to Sarel to think carefully of their Afrikaner heritage, their Afrikaner kultuur, the Afrikaner predominance in the area and the fact that he, LeRoux, was a member of the oldest Afrikaner family in the district. It was also time that there was an Afrikaner Mayor and, if their proud town's name was to be changed from its present Afrikaans, it should be to another Afrikaans name, like Rouxburg, for instance.

Mrs LeRoux was hustled off to the ladies' section of LeRoux Outfitters just as soon as her lord and master got home. Amanda chose for herself a rustling pink and purple taffeta creation that made her look like a bell tent at a Christmas party. She was intrigued, while surveying herself in the mirror, to observe the entrance of Mrs Drumpel and, shortly after her, Mrs van der Watt and Mrs Gruber.

For Sarel had had visits from Felix and van der Watt, who had stated their cases in no uncertain terms and had been given all the assurances they needed concerning who was to be the next mayor of 'Felicia' and 'Wattrus'.

Chapter 18

Saturday 28th January dawned bright and clear. When the sun took its first purposeful step over the eastern hills there were already many tired people at Boomplaas.

Bessie had been up since three a.m. and the kitchen bore pungent testimony to her industry. There were basins of curried fish and salads and platters piled high with cheese scones and *koeksusters.* Hams lay cooling under wire covers and ox tongues constricted slowly in basins beneath massive weights.

At the end of the lawn furthest from the house, trestle tables had been set up under the trees. Beyond them, in the clearing between the lawns and the tennis court, a huge pile of firewood grew with each visit by an enthusiastic *umfaan.*

The bonfires were set and on either side of them were large shallow drums into which coals from the fire would be shovelled before being covered with wire mesh in preparation for the cooking of yards of boerewors, *netvet* liver, and fat *pofadders.* There would be slabs of steak for the more conventional diners.

A pit had been dug and in it a great fire was already blazing. Over it were three spits which would carry the carcasses of fat young sheep, to turn slowly over the coals for about six hours and be ready by nightfall.

Coloured lights festooned the trees and spanned the lawns waiting for the throb of the diesel engine to bring them to life when darkness fell.

At nine thirty Bessie and Tina set off for town and a date with the hairdresser who had had to hire extra help and equipment from Koffiefontein in order to cope with the demand for her services.

Sarel and Spuds lowered themselves into deckchairs near the trestles and shouted to one of Kleinbooi's myriad grandsons to bring beer. Six huge tin baths were filled with crushed ice and dozens of cases of beer were already making pleasant tinkling noises as the ice shifted and melted slowly in the shade of the trees.

'Perhaps this will be the last great function here, Williams, my boy,' said Sarel and not even the beer could cloak the sadness in his voice.

'I don't think so, *Oom* Sarel.'

'An' just why?'

'You seem to have convinced yourself that Boomplaas must die and you must run away like a wounded old elephant to die far away!'

'What else can I do? I have never been one for half measures. This land is to produce mielies and wool, or oil, not both.'

'*Oom* Sarel, do you remember when we were first speaking about this, you asked me if I would like to be a farmer?'

'Yes, and you said no more than I would like to be an oil man.'

'Correct. Now I have a proposition to make to you and a request.'

'Go on.'

'I want you to give me a job as commercial manager of Boomplaas. This is my request. My proposition is that you become an oil man and I become a farmer.'

'You must be mad. I likes you very much Williams Mortimer, but to let you manage the farm would be the act of a fool. Almost as foolish as saying I know anything about oil.'

'No, man, you don't understand. Listen. You get the permit from the Minister to exploit the oil. I attend to the technical side of the operation and between us we make sure that it is all carried out with the minimum of damage to the farm. We do everything our own way at our own pace. It can work. I know it can. Then you can keep your farm and also satisfy your conscience.'

'An' how could you be happy to stay in this tiny platteland dorp when you have Johannesburg's fumes in your blood?'

Sarel looked closely at Spuds and saw the answer in the young man's eyes. Sarel was going to lose his granddaughter as well as his farm.

'An' what if I decide, after all, not to go for the oil, or if the Minister refuses the permit?'

'Then everything returns to normal.'

'I don't think Tina ever will.'

'Would you forgive me if I took her away from you?'

'I suppose it would be much too selfish to expect to keep both Boomplaas and Tina,' said Sarel wistfully.

Palmpoppiesfontein pulsed. By midday Lappies looked lovingly at emptied racks and shelves in his shop. The spurt of buying by the town's leading citizens had sparked off a chain reaction of feverish activity. The only shop to remain completely unpatronised was that of van der Watt. No one was going to do any eating until that night. Van der Watt did not mourn the lack of custom. Any loss he now suffered would be more than made up when he assumed the office of Mayor. The lull in trade had given him time to attend to his own needs in making himself as elegant as any borrowed plumes could effect on his pear-like torso.

Bisley's Pharmacy did a brisk trade in Alka Seltzer and sundry pain killing preparations. Judging by the quantity of other devices purchased that Saturday morning, the boys were going prepared for anything.

Inevitably the invitation list had grown as friends of friends pleaded to be included. Ultimately it became open house to the entire district.

Drumpel's Funeral Parlour was, fittingly, ignored. The very thought of anything as anti-social as death at a time like this was inconceivable.

Drumpel himself was no advertisement for his profession as he decked himself out in a flashy outfit complete with vivid tie. He even practised a few scintillating smiles, befitting a Mayor, in his wife's full-length mirror.

Gruber's Motors was strung with bunting and cars were being groomed on an assembly line basis. In anticipation of his Mayoral campaign, Heinz's customers were being presented with many objects of motoring use such as cool cushions, handy car trays and sets of matching tumblers.

If the populace were mystified by the exuberance of their leading citizens, they did not worry about it, but entered into the fiesta spirit with great abandon.

If the clamour of the main street had been a few decibels less, one could have heard the protesting rumblings and creaks of the doors of the Reformed Church as they gazed in horror at this unseemly frivolity, knowing as they did that it would escalate and spill over into the Sabbath whose holy dawn was but a few hours away.

The shops closed in exhaustion at one p.m. and the womenfolk went home to mudpacks and beauty sleeps, sitting up, of course, so as not to disturb the hair styles, now rigid with foul-smelling lacquers.

The menfolk pressed into the President Bar and proceeded to lay foundations for the evening. Bisley stood in his council chamber practising his inevitable acceptance speech which he knew would constitute the highlight of the evening. He was at pains to make it sound like an impromptu address.

'Dear citizens of our lovely town. Friends. You must forgive me tonight if I am a little incoherent. I came here to enjoy a social gathering with my friends – all of you (expansive gesture) – and now I am quite overwhelmed by your acclaim. I am at a loss for words to express my humble appreciation of the honour you have done me.

'However, I can, without high-sounding phrases, assure you, one and all, of my unswerving loyalty and attention to the glorious future of Palmpoppiesfontein ...' Then he practised a shy, self-effacing smile and a downward look. '... er, to be known henceforth as (impassioned gesture and heavenwards glance), '... oh, how can I merit it? ... Bisleyburg!' (Pause for wild clapping and cheering.)

Each run through the speech left Bisley more satisfied with his performance. He wished good old Rory could be there to view the dress rehearsal and perhaps polish up a phrase or two. But Morison was nowhere to be found.

In fact, he was in the middle of the crush in the President Bar, downing brandy after brandy, trying to drown a ridiculous doubt that kept jabbing at his mind.

Angus arrived, more by good luck than good navigation, at Boomplaas at about 2.30 that afternoon and settled himself near the drinks tables.

The smoke from the bonfire rose straight up into the still night air. The crackling of the flames mingled with the sizzling of the meat on the grids and the hiss of fat as it dropped from the spitted carcasses onto the glowing coals.

Over all was the hum of many voices and the tinkle of glasses. Those farmboys who had been unfortunate in the draw were now, instead of gorging themselves at Kleinbooi's kraal, squirming in unaccustomed fancy clothing of long white trousers and fancy red waistcoats. They had refused to squash their splayed feet into shoes and padded about with trays of drinks and platters of food.

Bisley mingled, acknowledging greetings with regal condescension. He was a trifle unsettled to see his councillors apparently copying his actions. Their dress was certainly not restrained and their womenfolk were decorated like queens. He hoped that his tasteful dark suit and his wife's navy blue outfit would be recognised as the product of taste and breeding. When he saw Amanda LeRoux in her abomination he was satisfied that no one in their right senses could fail to notice the difference between good taste and the lack of it. But it was with some concern that he saw little groups gathered around van der Watt, LeRoux and Drumpel. Heinz Gruber even rejoiced in a couple of acolytes.

Bisley did not like the gales of hilarity emanating from these groups at regular intervals, and he wished that Sarel would get on with his announcement so that things could fall into their right perspective and he could become the focal point of the evening.

He looked around for Rory Morison and saw him near the drinks tables. He went over to him.

'Rory, I've missed you today.'

He was answered by a loud 'hic' and some of Morison's brandy sloshed down Bisley's tie.

'Shorry, Tom, ol' boy. Been shelebratin'.'

'Oh..er..well..of course. I suppose I should be joining you.' He ordered a drink, alarmed that the usually dependable lawyer had reduced himself to a liability. Somehow he would have to be left out of the group photograph of the Mayor and council which Bisley had arranged to be taken immediately after Sarel's announcement and Bisley's acceptance speech. With approval he saw his photographer, surrounded by equipment, chewing a dainty piece of boerewors and sipping an innocuous tomato juice.

Sarel mingled with his guests and every now and then met Spuds and Tina at the beer drums to replenish tankards and discuss progress.

Everywhere the talk was of oil. Every group had its authoritative member who declared he knew the nature of Sarel's coming announcement. Preliminary deals were discussed and Spuds even heard Duvenage offer Koos van Lingen, Bessie's brother, a fantastic sum for his farm, Bessie's old home, which bordered on Boomplaas.

Tina came across Angus in the shadow of her tree.

'Hullo, Doctor. Enjoying yourself?'

'Immezhurably, m'deer. But no' half as much as I will a li'l later a'ter yer gramps has blown th' gaff!' He cackled. Tina was surprised to note that he was still quite steady on his feet. But there was a wicked gleam in his eye. Tina wondered what he was hatching.

Amanda LeRoux gathered a few close friends around herself and said conspiratorially, 'I just can't keep it to myself any longer. You know Sarel is going to give up the farm?'

'Yes?' they breathed expectantly knowing more secrets were to come.

'And,' continued Amanda, 'he told Bonatius that he wants him to be mayor!' Her glee communicated itself to the other ladies who hugged themselves in excitement.

'Me, Amanda LeRoux, mayoress of Rouxburg!' she said loudly.

Unfortunately she was standing back to back with Dorcas van der Watt of the accurate ashtray. Although half Amanda's size, she swung around to the attack.

'Indeed!' She looked the bell tent up and down in disgust. 'I think that as my husband is to be mayor of Wattsrus, it is reasonable to presume that I shall be mayoress!'

'You! Wattsrus! What nonsense!' shouted Amanda, beginning to quiver. 'Who ever heard of a grocer being a mayor?'

Dorcas shaped up to the taffeta mountain and began to hiss.

'Cheap hussy. Mayoress, my foot! They'd have to get an oxwagon to cart you to functions!'

The crisis which was developing was drowned in the sudden clamour of a brass bell which Spuds was ringing with much enthusiasm.

He stood under the bright light which had been erected near the verandah steps. He raised his arms. The silence was complete.

'Ladies and gentlemen, as you know there is an announcement to be made by Mr Labuschagne. If you would be so kind as to gather around here I will ask *Oom* Sarel to address you.'

Sarel made his way through the crowd and mounted the steps. Bisley sidled up to be near him and stood in the bright light. So did Lappies, Drumpel, van der Watt and Gruber. They glared at each other.

'My friends,' began Sarel, 'I wish to thank you all for coming here tonight and I hope that you will enjoy the party to the full. There is plenty to eat and drink.

'Now, you all know of the strong possibility that oil lies under these lands of Boomplaas. We are all aware of the great benefit this could be to our town and our country. You will also agree with me, I am sure, that to forfeit my farm and home would not be an easy decision to make.'

There was a great murmur, almost a huge sigh of sympathy. The crowd settled down and Sarel continued.

'After a lot of thought, I decided to exploit the oil ...' He was interrupted by shouts of 'good old Sarel' and much handclapping. Bisley beamed. Here it comes, he thought. Sarel held up his hands for silence.

'Now, my friends, you know me to be a man of deep convictions and, some tell me, of great stubbornness ...' Laughs crackled at him. '... I am also, I think, a man of great honesty and I expect this in others.'

'Of course, of course,' they all chanted.

Bisley saw Morison's smile slip and felt his own begin to slide as something cold clawed at his vitals. Sarel was speaking again.

'When I received an **order** from the mayor and council to stop wasting time and to do something about the oil, I was a little hurt that they should harass me so. After all my home is involved. When I received an ultimatum from them that invoked some section of the Law of the Land, which apparently would force me to dispose of my property, I was very angry.'

Faces hardened and a mutter started in the crowd, something about 'heartless swines who never give a chap a chance'. Sarel again held up his hands.

'But my personal anger was no reason to change my decision to develop the oil. In any case, it appeared that the law was still with the council and against me, and I therefore began to consider the best ways of exploiting the oil.'

Even Bisley brightened a little. All was not lost.

'Then came the great shock,' said Sarel, his voice hardening. 'I discovered that the council had been trying to force me to do something that, besides not being prescribed by the law, was in fact illegal.'

He went on to tell them, speaking louder and louder over the growing drone of dissatisfaction, of the correct interpretation of the ordinance and the constitution. '... and so,' he concluded, 'I can do nothing without permission from the Minister of Agriculture and, due to the handling of this matter,' he looked meaningfully at Bisley and his group, 'I do not feel inclined at present to apply to him for permission to prospect for oil.'

Bisley and his gang were rooted to the spot. The muttering of the crowd grew in volume. Bisley looked at Morison with hate and Morison merely grinned back at him in alcoholic abandon.

It would be difficult to say what would have happened if Angus had not thrown the tomato. It landed on Bisley's nose. This was the signal for the release of the tensions of the crowd, who saw in their councillors an oil-less, moneyless future.

When the mayoral party finally escaped in their cars they were covered from head to foot in curried fish and salads and everything else that the mob had been able to lay their hands on. Their scragging had been accompanied by the almost hysterical laughter of Angus McTiver, who pranced around the crowd, whooping, and taking pot shots at the councillors with his abundant supply of tomatoes.

It was Sarel and Spuds who finally managed to extricate the Mayor and Co. from the mob and bundle them into their cars.

When the last councillor's car had disappeared down the drive, a shamed silence descended. People stood around looking crestfallen, wiping their hand surreptitiously. Sarel again climbed the steps.

'I am sorry, my friends, that this has happened. It was most uncivilised of us all.' He had trouble keeping the smile off his face. 'However, I feel that justice has been done. I now want to appeal to you to exercise great care in the forthcoming elections. Oil or no oil, no town can hope to prosper if under the administration of self-seekers and fools. Give Palmpoppiesfontein the chance to develop its natural attractiveness, give it an energetic and unselfish council and, in due time all will benefit.'

'If I am satisfied that the town is in good hands, I may approach the Minister later this year to obtain the necessary permission to exploit the oil. The future is in your hands.'

They applauded him as he descended the steps and gathered around him, patting him on the back. Then they all had a final drink and went home.

Spuds found Angus fast asleep in a flower-bed and picked him up and put him to bed in a spare room in the farmhouse. Bessie and Sarel went off to bed and the lights went out. The moonlight washed softly over Tina and Spuds as they sat near the dying bonfire.

'Well, Tina, it's all over. It looks as if Boomplaas is safe.'

'Yes,' she sighed. 'And I suppose now you'll be going away?'
'I guess so. I've still to look at that asbestos at Jacobsdal.'
He stared into the fire.
'When are you coming to Johannesburg, Tina?'
'Oh, Willem, it will be very hard to leave *Oupa* now. This has been a terrible strain for him. We'll have to wait and see.'

Chapter 19

Spuds awoke to the jangling of the telephone bell. His room for the night had been in the front of the house near the hall and the telephone. He clambered out of bed and went to the phone.

'Is that Palmpoppiesfontein 2602?'

'I dunno. I suppose so,' mumbled Spuds sleepily.

'Hold on for Johannesburg.'

'Hullo? Hullo? Is that the farm Boomplaas?'

'Yes.' Spuds' head was sore.

'Is Mr Mortimer there? Mr William Mortimer?'

'Speaking.'

'William! Is that you?'

'Yes.'

'What's the matter, you sick?'

'No. Tired. Hangover.'

'Well, snap out of it. Rawlins here.'

Rawlins was the SPUDS chief geologist.

'Yes, sorry Mr Rawlins.'

'What's the position down there regarding the oil?'

'Flop. No oil. High yield farm.'

'Fine.'

'Huh?'

'I said fine. We won't have to worry about that bit of oil. Even if it is cleared for prospecting.'

'How was that again?'

'Look, William, go and have some breakfast and an aspirin and then go into town. Get the Sunday Times. Then I want you back here chop-chop.'

'What's all the excitement about?'

'You'll see in the paper.' There was a click as Rawlins hung up. Spuds replaced the receiver. Tina came sleepily down the passage in a pair of transparent shortie pyjamas.

'What is it Willem? I heard the phone?'

'I don't know yet. That was my boss. I must get dressed and go into town and buy the newspaper.'

'Wait for me Willem. I'll get dressed and come too.'

'You wouldn't consider staying as you are, I suppose?'

Tina stuck out her pink tongue at him.

The main street of the town was quiet. Business houses were shut.

The President Hotel looked ashamed of itself as it always did on a Sunday. The only house of commerce open was the corner café.

The church was open although it was at least two hours before the service was due to begin. The massive doors seemed to sneer in triumph at the tightly shuttered President's Bar. Spuds had the feeling however that attendance would be down this Sunday. On the other hand, the consciences of those who could summon the energy to attend would ensure the success of the collection plate.

Spuds went into the café and bought the paper. The headlines screamed at him.

SOEKOR STRIKES WITH A VENGEANCE

and in slightly smaller print: 'successful prospecting ensures steady oil flow for South Africa'. The first two pages of the paper were filled with the story.

Soekor had struck oil at Rustenburg in the Western Transvaal. The deposit was of such quantity that all available machinery and technical personnel of all affiliated industries had been co-opted to assist. All other prospecting would be banned in a special edition of the Government Gazette.

They sat in the shade of the Tina tree at Boomplaas. All traces of the night before had been removed. A cold lunch was set out on the trestle-table around which sat Sarel, Bessie, Tina, Spuds and Angus, who had no intention of going home until justice had been done to the party liquor.

'So, *Oom*, even if you wanted to mine you oil now, you couldn't.'

'Ag, man, I always said Boomplaas was for mielies and the Arabs for oil.'

'What about the tobacco farmers in Rustenburg where this oil has been found?'

'Pah!' Sarel spat. 'Tobacco! How can you compare such a farm with a sheep or mielie farm? An' those Vaalies are nothing but bloody Arabs anyway!'

They all laughed. Sarel was happy again. Boomplaas was safe. They could relax. After lunch, Spuds went inside, fetched his suitcase and put it in the boot of his car. He kissed *Tante* Bessie and shook hands with Sarel and Angus.

'Good bye, Williams Mortimer, you farmer's pest.' Sarel laughed at his own joke: too loudly, too long. They all looked at him closely but his expression was bland. Too bland.

Tina walked to the car with Spuds. He kissed her quickly and climbed into the car.

'Hey, *wat maak jy, man?* Tina, watchu doing now?' Sarel shouted.

'Why *Oupa*, what's the matter?'

Sarel turned and went into the house. He soon returned with another suitcase. Tina's.

'Get into the car, my girl,' he said. 'Your father's farm is near Rustenburg. It's time you went to see him. An' you can keep an eye on this Williams in case he tries to make monkeys out of those poor Arabs in the Transvaal.'

As the car topped the rise of the Trompsburg, Tina looked back. Boomplaas was a green splash on the reddish-brown canvas of the veld and, as the wind swirled down from the hills the trees swayed to its rhythm. The river winked and sparkled as it looped around the farm and then set off towards the distant town.

Palmpoppiesfontein was a brown smudge above which Tina could just make out the spire of the church.

As the car sped away towards Bloemfontein and Spuds took Tina's hand tightly in his own, Tina thought she could hear the church bells ringing and hoped that it was not her imagination.

The Helper

Paul Lehman

This story is true to the conditions and traditions of the early Transkei and reflects the difficulties of black people attempting to become urbanised in their quest for a better life. This terrible struggle is contrasted with the serenity of the rural life of the black people.

None of the characters exists except in the mind of the one who has drawn them out of his upbringing in their midst.

Chapter 1

The old man sat motionless against the mud wall of his hut. A shadow, cast by the rim of the thatched roof, darkened the top of his brown face and impressed the wrinkles as black lines. His hair, white and wiry, speckled his oval skull like fungus on a riverside stone. His eyes were closed, his breathing soft and hardly noticeable.

He sat in the sun that blazed down from the middle of the sky and generations, ages, centuries of living hovered around him. Through his sleeping mind fled vague, half-formed memories of things he had never seen. His blood, that stream of savagery, witchcraft and primitive art, coursed through his withered limbs with the vigour of an ageless youth: but he sat in the warmth of the sun and slept.

He slept while the *impi* yelled and charged endlessly, agelessly, dead but undying in his blood. About him pranced the spirits of the warriors, thrusting assegais and brandishing shields but never had there been a weapon in the old man's hand.

As the sun called the heat waves from the rocks and made them dance on the hardened earth, old Fakuwe leaned his back onto his wall, as he had done for many years now, and slept.

The women sang as they hoed the lands on the other side of the river. On Fakuwe's side, the ground, save for a small patch of browning maize, was bare. It was so because Ntsembu, his tired old wife, could no longer wield the heavy hoe for long hours in the heat of the day. Sometimes the young women from Mgulu's kraal across the river came over at the ford and helped Ntsembu for a day, but this was not often as Mgulu had much land for them to tend.

Fakuwe and Ntsembu were alone. For nearly ten years they had fought the soil for their livelihood, ever since the day the only son and only child, Dodane, had gone to work on the mines. He should have returned a number of times, bringing money for cattle and wives for himself, so that the kraal could flourish again. But, except for one letter some years before, they had heard nothing of him.

The soil calls for strength and youth in those who would master it and Fakuwe's arms were even weaker than those of his wife. The soil is a woman who calls for a man of strength that she may lose herself in his possession and bear him fruit in abundance as a tribute to his power.

Dodane's letter had been penned for him by someone who could write and it had been sent to the local trader, Van Deventer, who had read it to Fakuwe and Ntsembu and had explained the strange words to them.

The letter had told them of the wonders of iGoli, the great city of gold; of the lorries and trains and cars like the ants of the kraal; the huts so high that they disappeared into the clouds; the people whose numbers defied the fingers; the places to which one had to go, and even pay, to see some grass and not even be allowed to lie or walk on it. The letter had told them of other black men, from all over Africa, who spoke tongues strange to the Zulu and the Xhosa; the loneliness when one is among so many people; the happiness of making a friend.

Dodane's letter also told them of the back-breaking and dangerous labour deep in the heat and the darkness of the earth's belly, for the yellow stone that the white men prized so greatly; the penalties for the making and drinking of liquor; the hatred and fear of the police. All these things he had told them in the letter so many years ago. Now he could be dead.

On Fakuwe's visits to buy tobacco, if the trader was not too busy the letter would be read yet again. It was kept in the safe, in a position of honour with the trader's money. It would be taken out with much ceremony and Fakuwe would open it carefully. The mass of blue marks like so many insects scrambling across the paper made his eyes open in wonder and he would then breathe, 'Hau!' and hand the letter to the trader to be read. Then he would settle himself on the sacks of beans and maize and listen with rapt attention, to the words of his son, the helper, Dodane.

When the reading was over, Fakuwe would go to the front verandah of the shop and squat there with the other men. He would look out over the fields and the mielies, past the women working, beyond the *umtshotsho* boys coming over the hill. He would see beyond the huts on the hillside and his gaze would fix, though unseeing, on the distant sparkling sea.

He would think of Dodane of the strong arms, who would love the soil so that it bore him much fruit. Now his son laboured under the earth and took nothing from it but rock. While Dodane wasted his strength and youth on the yellow rock, the soil of Fakuwe's land grew hard and unyielding because old Fakuwe could not satisfy her.

After the reading Fakuwe would walk slowly home to Ntsembu and when he returned to his lands he would weep the deep salted tears of loss beyond understanding. As he walked along the dusty paths and saw the young *amantombi,* laughing with huge bundles of wood on their heads, his tired old eyes became filled with tears. His son could have chosen any of these, these beautiful young women, round of breast and hip, who would have borne him many children. But now Dodane only saw his people dressed in the discarded cloth of the whites, the young black women of the city more shameless than these, fresh of the fields, who walked with breasts bare and proud.

If his son had taken a wife in the city, they would be living in hovels among dirt and disease and other men would steal his wife for nights and she, being only a city girl, would aid the thief in his crime. Aau! Dodane! Why have you lost your soul for gold?

Home from the readings, Fakuwe would sit against the wall of the hut once more and the sun and his tears would lull him to sleep and Ntsembu would leave him to sleep away his sorrow all day. As he slept the spirits of the Xhosa kings enveloped him, infused his being and strengthened him. When the sun had cooled and dipped toward the western hills, Fakuwe would eat whatever Ntsembu had prepared for him.

Then they would close the door of their hut and build up the fire against the cold of the night. Fakuwe would tell his wife about the reading and the city that kept their son from his people. Ntsembu would do her best to comfort him, telling him that Thixo, the good God, would soon send their Dodane home.

Soon they would sleep while the wind blew chill over their fruitless lands and made the soil even harder against the two old ones.

Thus came and went the days of many years in the risings and settings of the sun and fullnesses of the moon. Fakuwe grew greyer and more wrinkled and the strength steadily deserted his old wife's arms. Each year the mielie crop diminished. Yet never did their hope fade. Resignation hung heavily upon them, but it did not deepen into despair.

Chapter 2

Dodane had an enquiring mind. At the age of seventeen, confined to a rural life, steeped in tradition, never having had any formal schooling, he had no introspective ability: he did not know what an enquiring mind was. He knew he was a *qaba* as most of the young men in the district were, but he was troubled by things he heard, often merely in eavesdropping on a conversation of the old men who spent much of their time on the verandah of the shop, smoking their long-stemmed pipes and philosophising in great serenity to reach agreement on the weighty matters pertaining to the soil, the cattle and the weather. But sometimes a newcomer, or a young man back from one of the big cities of the whites would enter the discussions and many troublesome things were heard.

The power of the paper money that some of his acquaintances brought back from iGoli and Imonti, the treasures that it could extract from Van Deventer's shelves and the swaggering walk that accompanied the donning of a new pair of trousers, all these crept, almost unbidden, into Dodane's wide open mind. The recognition of a life beyond the obvious stirred in his searching mind and soon his will began to assert itself demanding more knowledge and, subtly, more power than a *qaba* could expect to achieve no matter how many wives and cattle he might one day acquire.

He *umcho-cho'd,* drank beer and fought with sticks. He tended the cattle and the goats. Surreptitiously, because it would not be considered manly if he were seen, he even helped his mother to pound the mielies in the tall wooden pestle. After his circumcision a year earlier, he had flirted more meaningfully with the ever-willing, eager young *amantombi.* But none of this satisfied him fully. Often he felt as if he were on the outside, looking in, detached from the beer drink, the stick fight, the warm breasts in the reeds near the river.

Finally, he knew that he had to find out more about the world beyond the Amatolas. He went to the only source of information that he knew of, the trader, Van Deventer.

'*Inkosi* Van, how big are these *kraals* of the white man?'

'*iGoli*? *Imonti*? These *kraals,* Dodane?'

'*Ewe, Inkosi.*'

'They are not *kraals* like Mgulu's, Dodane, they are mighty cities where thousands of people live.'

'This much?' Dodane held up both hands, fingers outstretched and waved them back and forth to indicate counting in tens.

'No, Dodane, many, many times more than that. And there are huts so high they can touch the clouds.'

'And where do they keep the cattle and pigs?'

'Not in the cities, Dodane, only on the farms, like here in the Transkei. Then they take them to the cities to kill them for food.'

'Hau! Not for *lobola*?'

'No, Dodane, the white man's way of life is not like yours. Why do you ask these things?'

'Because I must know. I do not even know Butterworth or Kentani. But I must see this *iGoli* where they make the paper money.'

As the NRC agent, Van Deventer knew that the time had come to interest the young man in the fortunes and perils of the mines.

He thought the young man was perhaps not quite ready but his ambition and interest could not be diverted, of this the trader was sure.

'Dodane, you know that I am able to see to it that you are taken to *iGoli* to work on the mines, to dig for the gold and to be paid well, for it is hard and dangerous labour. Do you wish to go?'

'Yes, *Inkosi*, oh yes.'

'You must ask your father for permission.'

'He will grant it.'

'You must sign on for five years.'

'This I will do.'

On the day of the bus the passers-by on their way to the store took little or no notice of the young bucks who stamped and shouted and laughed and urinated into the bushes at the side of the road. Someone had a cheap concertina which wailed and squawked on three or four notes only. They sang the songs of their imagination, telling how they were going to tear down the mountains of gold and earn much paper money and then live like chiefs with women and cattle to their hearts' desire.

Occasionally a fight would break out and there would be curses and shouts and the clash of wild-lemonwood sticks and *knobkerries*, until the combatants rolled in the dust, laughing as their anger faded as quickly as it had arisen. A trickle of blood from a wounded head was of no concern to anyone.

That the bus was late was not an unusual event. The driver must have got himself drunk again and landed in the bed of one of his many female friends down at the coast. However, the train for East London only departed from Butterworth at seven o'clock in the evening, so there was plenty of time to waste, if it could be counted as a waste of time to laugh and play and shout lewd, but sometimes accepted, suggestions at the passing *amantombi.*

The trader came out of his store every now and again with a list of names, checking that his current batch had all arrived. At a healthy fee per head, recruiting was a lucrative by-product of his central function in the district.

Above the verandah roof of the shop was a large poster, depicting a young Xhosa in mineworker's uniform. It was as glamorous to Dodane and his companions as the call of the South African Air Force was to the white youths of their age.

The young blacks would sign on for terms of labour, returning home between contracts to plough, buy cattle or marry wives and gradually set up kraals of their own. Then, if they had not become too embroiled in the life and lure of the city, they would eventually return to the lands of their fathers and live the lives of gentlemen, while their womenfolk tended the soil and bore them many children, preferably daughters, as they earned *lobola.*

At last the bus arrived in a cloud of dust, a series of backfires and the clattering of badly worn pistons. The vehicle seemed full already, but still the mine recruits clambered aboard. Their pitifully small bundles of possessions were thrown onto the roof racks together with the assortment of boxes and crates and cheap suitcases, blanket rolls and wire mesh cartons containing fowls and ducks which added to the din.

Venting his splenetic headache on the machinery under his control, the driver set off in a clashing of gears, accompanied by a roar of farewells from the crowd.

In the bus, the clamour of voices battled above the racket of the engine and the incessant crashing of the sliding windows, loosened beyond repair by the weekly trips over a road that should not have rejoiced in such a name at all: in winter it resembled the dry bed of a river and in summer it became a quagmire of red and black mud for every inch of its thirty miles, before it finally joined the main road to Butterworth.

The passengers sang and shouted, blew and sucked their mouth organs. Mothers exposed melon-like breasts and fed their squalling infants while a smuggled piglet yelled its discomfort in the back corner of the bus into which it had been thrust. Packed like sardines, the passengers swayed and jolted, jerking in every direction as the kamikaze driver hurled his agonised bus over boulders, through rain-made trenches and across potholes which seemed even bigger than the wheels themselves. Hairpin corners were taken at full speed without regard for the precipitous drop into the valleys far below.

A group of youths beside the road ran wildly from the approaching bus, heading for a small grass hut on the hillside. They wore white blankets and their faces and bodies were smeared with white ochre. They ran away because they were not supposed to be seen by anyone until their initiation days were over. For they were *abakhwetha*, young men living in seclusion and undergoing instruction before being circumcised and presented to the community as men.

They lived together in their little hut for about two weeks with an instructor who taught them the secrets of life and love and their tribal traditions. Then they submitted to the assegai of the witchdoctor who then bound up each mutilated penis with herbs and the leaves of aloes. No flinching or cry of pain was allowed if the youth was to emerge from the initiation as a man.

The occupants of the bus laughed and jeered at the scampering figures as the vehicle tore past them, covering them with dust.

Seeing them, Dodane recalled his own initiation, only two years earlier. The pain had been excruciating as manhood seemed to demand a very high price. Now his penis looked as if it had been chewed by a rat: their witchdoctor was getting on in years and was not particularly steady of hand and blade.

Dodane remembered Notemba, his first, and their meeting in the reeds near the river. It had not been her first, that he knew, but it had been his. And it had been all too soon after his man-making. The pain and the pleasure had been so closely entwined that he could not remember them clearly as different sensations.

He had never recaptured that first orgasm of so many feelings. Perhaps in Johannesburg there would be some women who would be able to help him to the heights of complete satisfaction ... perhaps the white man who turns rocks into gold had been able to teach the black people some of this art as well.

Butterworth lay in a hollow and sweated. Dust turned into mud on the faces of those venturing onto the street. Trees, greyed by dust, drooped in the windless heat. But, as the bus rattled down the main street of the village and turned down towards the station, Dodane did not notice the heat at all. He was entranced. Although the buildings were only one storey in height, they were impossibly large. There were huge flat plates of glass and many motor cars. How could people have so many things?

On one corner of the main street there was a most impressive building, also with no thatch on its roof, and a large sign on its wall said HOTEL. Dodane nudged one of his companions and said, 'What is that? What does that name say?'

'It is a place where people go to drink and sleep and eat,' was the reply. 'They pay there instead of eating and sleeping at their own hut.'

'Is there beer there?'

'Yes, for the white man.'

'Can we not get beer there?'

'No, we must not drink white man's drink. Only our own beer, what they call kaffir-beer is permitted.'

'But if we have the money, why can't we buy beer?'

'If you as much as step inside that place the police will throw you into the jail.'

'Hau!' said Dodane. 'Anyway, in *iGoli* it will be different.'

The railway line had never traversed the Transkei completely. To go by rail from Butterworth to any other point in the country, one had to take the train to East London and then another to one's destination. In the opposite direction, the line went as far as Umtata, the capital, in the heart of the Transkei. From there to Durban or other parts of Natal, a railway bus was available.

The mine recruits poured out of the bus, grabbed their belongings and ranged through the village, full of exuberance and excitement at their coming adventure. They gathered outside the only café in the village and sang and danced and spat in the dust until the fat Greek rushed out from behind his counter and chased them away in a torrent of abuse. For the rest of the day he fulminated and mourned the loss he must have suffered because for half an hour no one had been able to enter his shop.

At last the time came to board the train: a great enough excitement in itself. What wonders were to come? During the night the train wound its way down through the Kei hills and the cuttings in the steep sides of the valley walls. It crossed the Kei river by means of a bridge used by both cars and trains and then followed the long, puffing, wheel-spinning pull up to the Ciskei flats before the clacketing downgrade to the coast and finally, at seven o'clock in the morning, the triumphant, steamy entrance into the station at East London.

The newcomers were not too sure of themselves in this totally new world and did not venture far away from the station and at midday they boarded the express train to Johannesburg, packed into their bare wooden third class carriages of the terrifying, shrieking, rushing monster that bore them away from their roots.

Ahead of them lay long years in the depths of the earth. Armed with lights and picks and shovels, they would be going down into the heat and smell and the noise of the shuddering jackhammer; the bowel-loosening terrors of the swift-falling cage and crashing rock; the darkness and the raw fear of the unknown.

They would soon forget the green of the mielies and the grass, the lowing of cattle, the song of the river.

Chapter 3

When the train jolted and screeched to a stop on platform 14, Dodane looked out onto a new world far beyond what he had expected. There was no grass, there were no huts, no mielies, no cattle. Instead of the gurgle of the river threading its way through the stepping stones, there was the blare of metallic voices shouting incomprehensible words out of boxes tied onto poles. Instead of the blue and white of a wind-teased sky, there was a heavy blanket of grey overhead. The offensive smell of oil and hot metal replaced the living odours of fresh dung and woodsmoke.

'This is *iGoli*, the city of gold?' Dodane said to the man next to him, peering out of the compartment window.

'It must be, but the gold must be elsewhere,' was the reply.

'There is certainly no rock here, just as there is no soil or grass. How do people live with no lands?'

'These people live only for the paper money. They have no interest in the things of the soil. This my brother has told me. He has been on the mines for five years already.'

'And is he to return to Transkei, to his lands?'

'No. My father is sad, but my brother has been caught up in the white man's love of the paper. He now lives here.'

'This will not happen to me,' Dodane said with great conviction in his voice, 'I am of my people. I will take the paper money back to my father.'

They clambered from the carriages wherein for twenty-four hours they had sat on hard wooden benches, sleeping when they could against the shoulder of the man beside them. During the morning, when the train clattered through the Free State and southern Transvaal, they had marvelled at the huge tracts of mielie lands that stretched as far as they could see on either side of the track.

'Surely this is too much land, too many mielies for one man?' they had said to each other.

They stood on the platform with their blanket rolls beside them. A lucky few had battered old cardboard suitcases which defined them as seasoned travellers, but still this *iGoli* was full of fear for them all. Their apprehension increased when they were approached by an awesome black man dressed in a magnificent khaki uniform. He even wore a majestic peaked cap with a brown metal badge in the front and the peak of the cap was red! They were plunged into a confusion of emotions when the man began to speak to them and they realised he was a Zulu.

'You are the recruits from Butterworth?' he stated more than asked.

'*Ewe*,' they chanted in unison.

One of them, a little more adventurous said '*Yebo*' and the great man rounded on him swiftly. '*Ewe* will do from you jackals of Xhosa. I know your tongue but don't you attempt to defile mine with your mouth. Now you must pick up your *impahla* and follow me. Outside in the street you will see a large truck. Get onto the back of it and stay there until I tell you to get out.'

He stalked away proudly and the young bucks, very chastened, followed him closely not wanting to be lost in this maelstrom of people. There were people everywhere. Dodane had never seen as many people, certainly never so many white people.

Their clothes entranced him and he looked down in disgust at his own tattered trousers and broken shoes. His companions looked and felt no better as they trudged along behind the huge angry Zulu.

As they passed the big black locomotive at the end of the platform it hissed and clanked at them adding to their fright and bewilderment. The driver and his stoker leaned over the side of the cab and grinned at the motley bunch of black youths. 'Ja you black bastards, now you'll find out what work is. *Geniet dit*!'

Dodane stored this away in his receptive mind. Why did they speak in such a harsh tone to them? He could not understand the words, but the tone was unmistakeable.

They climbed hurriedly onto the back of the open truck, still fearful of being left behind, abandoned, in this huge, ugly, noisy, stench-laden place. As they travelled through the midday streets of Johannesburg, their awe increased until they were beginning to doubt the evidence of their eyes.

The motor cars were like ants on a food sortie. They stopped suddenly when a red eye glared at them while ants came from a different direction, then when the eye became green once more, they hurried away. The people ran in between the cars and did not seem to take any notice of the coloured eyes. Even the yellow one, which seemed to make all the ants hesitate, did not deter the people who hurried along, grim faced, intent and unaware of those around them. Did they never stop to pass the time of day? To talk? To enquire about each other's health? Dodane was amazed to see the black people, of whom there were so very many, dressed like the whites and also lost in the rush of their progress from one place to another.

The huts were so tall and had so many glass eyes that Dodane could not understand how they stayed upright, because the mud of the walls should have cracked under their own weight. And, most disturbing of all, although they had been driving for a long time, there was still no sign of grass, or crops, or water, or cattle, or anything that could be honestly described as a tree. Hau! How could anyone live in such a barren place?

Their spirits lifted somewhat on their arrival at the mine compound. There was some grass and a large pool of blue water in which they were told they could swim. They were given stiff new uniforms and wonderful hats with lights on top of them and then shown to large dormitories which were to be their homes. Their first meal at the communal eating hall was another surprise in its quantity and quality.

They were told the details of their pay and how the mine would save a portion of it on their behalf and pay it to them with extra *basela,* something for nothing, when they finally drew their money to go home.

All these wonderful things were forgotten when, after a period of tuition on the ground, they made their first plunge into the bowels of the overheated earth. How could anyone survive the noise and the heat and how, in the name of *Thixo,* could anyone hope to rise once more to the surface of the world.

Dodane was quick to differentiate between the classes and grades of workers and he made up his mind from the very first day that he was going to be a 'boss boy' in the shortest time possible. He also realised, after but a few weeks, that overtime and the more dangerous jobs paid considerably more money, and therefore were to be sought in order to amass as much of the paper money as possible in the time he would have.

On his first day off, accompanied by some of his friends, he braved the unknown terrors of the strange buses. Ignorant of direction and relying on the assistance and advice of other black passengers, he made his way to Soweto, the black city on the outskirts of Johannesburg.

He wanted a woman and he wanted to drink and the former was no problem at all. A minimum of finesse and hypocrisy was involved and he had soon attached himself to a buxom young woman who led him to a nearby *shebeen.* He had been warned about the illegality of these places and, although he could not understand what all the fuss was about, he decided to be sensible until he knew more about the laws and restraints of living alongside the white man.

After he had temporarily quenched the build up of desire over the many weeks since leaving home, he lay on his back on Tsilinga's rumpled bed and asked her for a cigarette. She rummaged around and finally gave him a brown paper tube which she lit and placed in his mouth. He instantly recognised the smell and taste of dagga, the African hashish which he had occasionally grown and enjoyed himself in a corner of his father's land.

'Dodane,' she said, 'this too, like the liquor, is forbidden by the police. Do not let them find any of it on you.'

'Is there any end to the laws against us, Tsilinga?'

'It would seem not. We are forbidden most things and always remember that your pass is the most precious thing you have.'

'Do the white men carry passes as well?' he asked.

'No. The whites do as they wish. They can even go and live elsewhere in the country without permission from anyone.'

'And we? Can we do so?'

'No. When your contract at the mine is over, or if they dismiss you for drunkenness or stealing, you have to go back to where you came from. No other course is open to you.'

'Aau! But my peoples' cattle have more freedom than this!'

'Ewe, *mfondini*, yes, my friend. We are slaves.'

'Can you read and write, Tsilinga?'

'Yes. Xhosa and Afrikaans. I was educated at a Dutch Reformed mission station near Queenstown.'

'Now why would they teach a slave to read and write?'

Tsilinga thought about this for some time. Dodane was no ordinary man; his questions were strange.

'Perhaps they need slaves for duties other than digging and cooking and breaking rocks?'

'No. I would only teach my slaves to obey the whip. There is more to this mission schooling than we can understand. Will you write for me to my father?'

'Of course. Tell me the words and I will write.' She rose and fetched a pen and some paper.

And so was written the first and only letter that Fakuwe received from his son. The letter that lay in its place of honour in Van Deventer's safe between the ritual readings.

Dodane sat beside Tsilinga on the untidy bed in the cold ceilingless room and watched in wonder as she took the words out of his mouth and made them into lines and circles on the paper. Then she read back to him what he had said to his parents, folded the paper and put it into an envelope. She addressed it and told Dodane how much in stamps to stick onto it. In awe he took the envelope and looked at his father's name. 'Fakuwe Qolotoke', strange in the flickering candlelight, looking like a blue worm sleeping on the paper.

'It is a wonderful thing to be able to write, to make paper speak for you,' he said. 'This is something that I must learn.'

'You will have to go to night school,' she said. 'See if there is one at the mine.'

'You think they will teach me all these things as well as how to get the gold?' he asked doubtfully.

'Oh yes, I am sure. And you should learn quickly. You are not an ordinary *qaba* and learning is a good thing. Too few of our people have knowledge. You are the prey of everyone if you know nothing. You cannot even see if you have been given the correct change when you buy. Our people can never become anything until we have wise blacks who can speak for us.'

'But the white man must know this? So why should he help us to become his equals?'

'We may become his equals in the schoolroom, but he still makes and enforces the laws. We could for ever be slaves, even if educated.'

'From where do you have such ideas, Tsilinga. How can you expect the black man to become as wise as the white man, or as powerful?'

'I do not know, Dodane, but I have heard strange things that mean that one day we will be as free as we were before the whites came. At school there were those who told us that one day, soon, the Xhosa and the Zulu, and other tribes, would be returned to their homelands, such as Transkei and Zululand and these lands would be ours alone, free of the laws and wishes of the white government.'

'And what would we do with them?' he asked.

The girl looked at him speculatively. This is a strange man, she thought; he seems to think in angles instead of straight lines.

'Come,' she said, 'let us lie together again before you must return to the mine.'

As he made his way through the dark alleys of the township and during the long bus ride back to the mine, Dodane thought deeply about what had happened that evening and he felt frustrated at his lack of understanding. He knew he would soon learn to read and write but all these other unknown things that came from the world of the white man were something else. The only white man he had known, to speak to, up to now had been the trader *Inkosi* Van and already Dodane could see that the trader was far from representative of the white man.

He had been thrust from utter simplicity to a complexity of life that defied his logic. He was totally unequipped to cope with the most basic of needs, the ability to communicate. He resolved to rectify that with no delay at all.

Dodane did not expect the enthusiasm with which the mine personnel officer received his request to attend night school. He could not understand why anyone should waste time and resources training a rock breaker for anything else. However, he could not distrust the fact that forms were filled in and books were given and times of classes explained.

'Dodane,' the officer said, 'remember that schooling is in your free time, off shift, and if you want to learn quickly and well, there will be little time for anything else.'

'I must learn,' the young black man said with such ferocity that the officer was taken aback. Dodane's furious approach continued unabated for two years during which time he mastered English and Afrikaans as well as an ability to write his own language, Xhosa. He became intensely interested in Geography and History and his zeal and his searching questions both excited and disturbed his teachers.

At the same time he mastered the requirements of a team leader in underground work and became the youngest 'boss boy' the mine had ever known.

However, Dodane was still dissatisfied. The more he learnt, the more he became aware of the amount there was to be learned and just how vast were the gaps and voids in his knowledge. When his reading ability introduced him to the wonders of the daily press he developed an insatiable thirst for knowledge and understanding of the white man's politics. He saw that the white men were divided against each other seemingly just as passionately as they were distancing themselves from the black man. The Afrikaner had fought his way up from poverty, poor education and lack of culture and was now the force in governing the land. The English speakers, both immigrant and South African born, were far too obsessed with the accumulation of wealth and the promotion of business. They were too short-sighted to realise that political power was far more practical and all embracing as it had the ability to control even the development of the economy. The English speaking businessmen played right into the hands of the politicians who gave them all the rope they needed until the new breed of Afrikaans businessmen, well educated and belonging to the right party, from the correct universities and church, were ready to take their place in competition.

But what was of most interest to Dodane was the politics of black/white relationships. He questioned everything about the relative ways of life. He was too intelligent to waste his time on daydreaming about material possessions and wondering how he could also live in a fine house in Houghton. He knew that levels of material life existed, even at home. Mgulu was so much better off than Fakuwe – some had to labour with their hands others with their heads. The question that Dodane kept asking of himself and others was why blackness of skin meant a different set of laws.

He was puzzled by the somewhat sheepish reluctance with which his teachers tried to steer around the politically-oriented questions which he began to ask.

'Dodane, your question is about today's government, but this a history lesson; we are learning about the Great Trek.'

'But why must history be only of what is past?' Dodane replied.

'We should be making history now. My forefathers fought your forefathers and it seems to me that we are still fighting today, not with assegai and spear and gun, but with words. And to me it seems that our forefathers' deaths were more honourable, to both white and black, than this living death of rules which make no sense.'

After the lesson the teacher called Dodane aside and said, 'Listen, you must be careful of what you say in public places like the schoolroom and other places where there are many people. It is my task to teach you subjects which will help you to pass exams, no more than that. If you wish to become political, do it elsewhere but remember, the police have informers everywhere and once your name is in their files your life will become a hell.'

'But this is exactly what I am asking about. Why must the police be interested in me because I question the ways of life in my own country? I am not a revolutionary. I am a student.'

'Dodane, even white students who question the government and the laws get into trouble. A black student has no hope whatsoever. Stick to your English grammar and the geography of Europe. Finish your contract, take your money and go home.'

'Never! I have forgotten the grass and the river, the mielies and the cattle. I must continue to learn and to have my questions answered.'

Chapter 4

Dodane's moment of vision came during his third year at the mine. It came in the form of a mine accident, in itself comparatively unimportant, but in its consequences an opportunity for Dodane to reduce to its essentials the questions that haunted his burgeoning intellect.

A new area on a level far beneath the earth's surface had recently been opened up and prepared for excavation and development. A working team of three white miners and a gang of 'boys' under Dodane and in the control of a white shift foreman, Du Toit, were sent in on the first stage.

The hoist dropped, seemingly endlessly, into the increasing heat of the earth. When the cage was finally still after bouncing at the end of the extended cable, the workers climbed out and proceeded through the old workings and down a ramp into the new section.

They were clearing the working area and preparing the jackhammers to attack the new vein when suddenly they heard a loud rumbling. Their experienced ears told them that this was no ordinary or remote rockfall. Du Toit hurried to the far side of the area and pressed his ear to the rock surface. He heard the anger behind the vertical face of the rock and his hand quivered under its shuddering. Even as he shouted to his gang to get out, back up the incline to the old workings, Du Toit saw the rock face begin to bulge and crack. As he raced away in the wake of the others the rock erupted before a torrent of seething water. Before he could reach the incline the water tore at his feet and a piece of rock struck him on the head. Limp and senseless, his body was snatched up by the water and dashed against the opposite wall of the new chamber.

Horrified, Dodane, the last up the slope along which all the others had already scampered to safety, saw Du Toit disappear under the deepening dirty flood. He ran back down the slope and flung himself into the water, now a whirlpool formed by the inrushing water circling the walls of the chamber with increasing force.

He thrashed around in the gloom and finally caught a glimpse of the foreman. He managed to grip the man's heavy belt and fought his way out of the maelstrom of water, swallowing and spitting and gasping with the effort. When he reached the slope he heaved the unconscious man over his shoulder and struggled up the ramp away from the whirling water that heaved and sucked and hissed at his heels.

Realising what had happened, the others hurried back to help him just as he could carry his burden no longer and collapsed at their feet.

'... and you are all brave men,' said the mine manager to the crowd assembled before him. 'To travel far beneath the earth, to labour in its heat and ever present danger, is not something that can be done by ordinary men.

'We try to ensure your safety with the best of equipment and costly maintenance programmes but we are not perfect. We pay the highest possible wages, the least we can do, perhaps, in return for the type of labour that you give. But we live in danger and on those occasions when the possibility of danger becomes a reality and the earth threatens lives in a mine accident, then even the bravest of you can not be blamed for doing all in his power to save himself before anyone else.

'No one understands better than us miners, the instinct of self preservation and the strength of the force of fear. So, when we find a man forgetting his own safety and going to the assistance of his fellow worker, then we must acknowledge bravery of the highest order. And, when we have the instance, as now, of a black man saving a white man from certain death, then we know without doubt, that miners are a race apart, a brotherhood knowing no barriers. Bravery has nothing to do with the colour of a man's skin, neither has brotherly love.'

The applause was deafening as Dodane came forward to receive a medal and a cheque. Many newspaper photographers were there as he shook hands with Du Toit and the manager's speech was translated into Zulu, Xhosa and Sotho for the benefit of those without English.

Dodane could not forget the manager's words. They troubled him and annoyed him. The concepts conjured up by the speech were strange to him, but too complicated to isolate and think about logically. He had been introduced to the meaning of paradox without knowing the word itself. Initially without resentment, only puzzlement, he found himself comparing the 'brotherhood with no barriers' to the strict segregation of the white and black workers and the widely differing ways of life that they enjoyed. The white men had cottages on the mine property and their families lived with them. No black worker could have a woman of any relationship in his quarters. If we are brothers, he thought, why are we so different?

The speech also insinuated strangeness in the fact of a black saving a white. This perplexed him. Would a white then, not save a black? And if in fact he would, but such action was confined to miners only, what of all the other people in the city, the country, the world? Was he to understand that there was a gulf between black and white that normally could not be bridged?

Although there had never been any talk of wages, or comparison with the whites' earnings, Dodane now wondered how the danger could be compensated on different scales if the matter in question was the loss of life, as precious to Dodane or Du Toit as to anyone else.

He knew now, without any doubt, that he had arrived at the point where questions and the pursuit of their answers was to be the purpose of his life.

One evening, soon after the accident, Dodane went off shift and made his way into the northern suburbs. He had been a regular visitor, spending the night with Tsilinga, to the house where she worked in the home of a well-to-do white family.

This evening he was so preoccupied with his new search for the truth that he forgot the ritual of tossing a bone to the household's guard dog. However the dog knew him well enough to let him pass unmolested but the animal's disgruntled snort did not go unnoticed.

Dodane sat on Tsilinga's bed beside her and told her about the accident and the speech and the award. He told her about his anger at his inability to understand the implications of the words of the speech. He told her how his teachers steadfastly refused to enter into anything resembling a political discussion or even an explanation of any of the laws which Dodane could not accept.

'If we are so useful to them and this country,' he demanded, 'why are we treated so differently to the whites? Perhaps we are not clever enough or educated enough to be lawyers and bankers and doctors but it seems to me that we play a very large part in the prosperity of this land, by our labour. So why can we not be citizens?'

'They say,' replied the girl, 'that we do not belong here, in places like Johannesburg. They wish to create homelands for us to live in and to rule ourselves.'

'Hah! And who will break their rocks and carry out their rubbish bins and sweep their streets?'

'People like you and me, who will be allowed into the white man's towns to work but never to have any rights other than what we can achieve in our own lands.'

'And who is to say which land is theirs and which ours?'

'This is already ordained. The white politicians will give and take away as they please.'

Tsilinga could see that this line of talk was making Dodane angry and that he would lose interest in the reason for his visit whereas she longed for his strong arms and fierce sexual demands.

'Come,' she said with a laugh, 'let us go and lie on the madam's bed!' She laughed at his startled expression. 'They have gone out,' she explained and took him by the hand.

They left the cold eight-by-ten cheerless room and crossed the back garden of the property and entered the rear door of the double-storeyed house. Upstairs they threw themselves on the great double bed in the master bedroom and made violent love.

When they were spent they drank some of the master's whisky, tidied up the bed, topped up the whisky bottle with water and went downstairs where Tsilinga let Dodane out of the front door asking him to return soon.

Tsilinga went back upstairs to check that no sign of their presence on the bed remained. As she entered the room she stopped still in shock. There on the floor next to the bed was a small brown book, dog-eared and dirty, but instantly recognisable to the girl as Dodane's pass book.

She drew in her breath in fear as the frightening possibility of Dodane being picked up by the police, without a pass, struck her like a blow.

Dodane ambled along, deep in thought, towards the stop where the buses reserved for blacks picked up their passengers. He would be in time for the last bus to the West Rand. As he approached the stop he became aware of a vehicle drawing up beside him and he recognised it immediately as a cruising police van, complete with a reinforced wire cage over the load bed and two uniformed young constables.

They sprang out of the cab and came up to him telling him to stop, which he did, secure in the knowledge that he had done no wrong.

'Pass book!' The constable held out his hand peremptorily. Dodane reached into his back pocket and withdrew his hand and looked at it as if he could not believe its emptiness. The constable repeated his demand and moved closer, loosening the flap of his revolver holster. Frantically the young black man searched his other pockets and felt the fear creeping into his bowels. How could he have lost his permit to live, albeit in what he was beginning to look on as slavery. He shook his head at the policemen.

'I am so sorry, my baas, it seems I have lost my book!'

'Did you ever have one, *swartgat*?'

'Oh, yes, my baas. I know I had it an hour ago when I was visiting my friend in Houghton.'

'You have rich friends, kaffir?'

'No, my baas, just the girl who works for the white master.'

'Visiting the girl eh? You mean using her to make more black bastards like yourself!'

'I am black, yes, my baas, but I am not a bastard. My parents are married and live in the Transkei.'

'*Eina*, Neels,' constable one said to constable two with a grin on his thick-lipped mouth, 'here we have a smart kaffir. I think he is too clever for us. We will have to take him down to the Square for some questions, né?'

'*Beslis, ou maat, gooi die vellie in die kattebak.*'

Without further ado they literally threw Dodane into the back of the van and went on their way. During the rest of the night they cleared a large area of the select suburbs, eliminating potential 'criminals' whose major crime was the lack of government-approved identification.

In the early hours of the morning, their vehicle filled with blacks: some drunk, some injured, some drugged, some bewildered but all of them frightened, the two policemen called it a night and reported in to their charge office while their sorry cargo wearily clambered out of the van and unprotestingly allowed themselves to be herded into the cells.

When Dodane's turn came to be questioned he again explained that he had a pass and that it had been on his person that night, but must have been mislaid during his visit. His story received the same credibility that it had the night before and, when he came before the magistrate he was not even questioned in the court. The magistrate read the charge sheet and wearily waved him away to jail for three months.

However, Tsilinga became worried when Dodane did not appear for a week and she found her way to the mine and to a responsible official who listened to her story and took possession of the pass book.

The personnel manager of the mine was most concerned about the fate of their recent hero and managed to trace Dodane and arrange for him to be released. He explained who this black man was and convinced the authorities of the man's legal presence. Dodane was relieved to be released but his anger, already at boiling point because of his treatment, was fuelled even further by the parting remark of the policeman who returned his possessions to him.

'Hell, man, why didn't you tell us who you are? You saved a white man's life. You must be a good kaffir, *jong*.'

Dodane stored this away in his heart and soon realised that while it was wise to fear the police, it was far more pleasant and practical to hate them. And this he did for the rest of his life.

Chapter 5

The dust rose thickly to settle on glistening black arms, chests and backs and straining faces of the dancers, and rivulets of sweat streaked through the fine, grey powder on their bodies. The ground shook as the pounding feet thudded in unison. Assegais flashed in the sun. The leading man's piercing whistle shrilled continuously, demanding obedience from the leaping, swirling, shaking, rushing dancers.

Leopard skins and lion manes covered their loins. Beads covered legs from ankle to knee and hissed and chattered as the feet moved. Headdresses of horns and feathers swayed and jerked as seemingly boneless necks gyrated.

Audible above all the noise was the guttural grunting of the dancers. Frightening were their trumpeting yells as they leapt high into the air before slamming their cowhide shields onto the earth and leaping up again.

On a raised platform sat a visiting film star and her retinue. Behind her dark glasses, her normally tired, bored eyes sparkled as the excitement and savagery of the dance communicated itself to her. This was a new experience for her jaded senses.

The dance area was surrounded by spectators: the blacks noisy, vociferous, shouting at each other and the dancers; the visiting whites silent, wide-eyed, a trifle apprehensive; the compound manager and the other mine-working whites who had seen it all so often, though vaguely amused, were bored.

'Old Zingazi is certainly showing off today,' said one, as the leader of the dance cavorted and performed a prodigious leap.

'He seems to know when there's someone watching who will really be impressed. I bet he has already worked out how much of a tip he can extort from that silly little bitch,' replied another, waving his hand in the direction of the film star.

'These bloody nigs are like pet dogs or spoilt kids.'

'And some tit in Parliament is shouting that they should have a vote!'

'They wouldn't know what to do with it if they got it!'

'Ja, that's where the commies would get in and show the poor buggers where to make their cross.'

The dance appeared to be nearing its climax. The squealing whistle was insistent, the dancers' feet were planted firmly on the ground but their bodies vibrated vertically, muscles rigid and rippling like oil-slicked waves. The grunting was faster, more urgent, louder. The shaking of the glistening bodies became even faster, then the feet started to shuffle in the dust.

Suddenly, with a mighty yell that startled even the experienced watchers, the dancers leapt as one, high into the air and then rushed at the dignitaries' platform, drawing back assegai-wielding arms. They stopped a few feet from the dais and made as if to fling the spears, but, instead of releasing them, they jabbed them into the earth at their feet, falling to the ground themselves with knees and faces in the dust.

There was a hushed silence. The film star's hand was in front of her gaping mouth. Her face was ashen. At the assegai rush of the dancers she had uttered a frightened four letter word not associated with ladies and had felt her blood, so recently warming her loins, rush to her feet. Then, when she realised that she was not going to be stabbed or raped, she smiled again, a wan grimace, and began to clap daintily, a gesture soon followed by all the other spectators.

The dancers arose and saluted by slamming their assegais onto their shields and ran out of the arena.

Dodane turned to the black man beside him. 'These Zulus can certainly dance better than us Xhosas, but I don't know that they are any better otherwise.'

The man to whom he had addressed this observation was dressed in the stock outfit, give or take a few colours, of the well-to-do black man about town. Not the professional man of whom there were a pitiful few who dressed well even by white standards, but the gambler, tout, pimp and general troublemaker. He was a small man with a large head on which rested a huge, wide-brimmed navy blue hat. His suit was a loud check in yellow and brown, his shirt orange and his tie green. Red socks disappeared into tan shoes with white spats.

'They are nothing but barbarians,' the small man replied. 'This dance is savage, ridiculous. I have heard that when they urinate after dancing like this they pass pure blood!'

'Barbarians?' queried Dodane. 'And you yourself? You are black, you must be one as well?'

'Not at all,' he replied with a laugh. 'I am educated and civilized. I was born and brought up here in Johannesburg. I have never been tribal.'

'So you have had the benefit of the white man's ways since birth?' asked Dodane.

'That's correct. Is it not evident in my appearance and my speech?'

'I must say I have seen few white men as colourful as you. But do you mean to say that you think tribal blacks are savages and city born ones can throw off this savagery in one generation?'

'It is only a question of environment and circumstance. It is really only on the surface that the whites are what they call 'civilized'. The only difference between white and black savagery is that ours is more basic, more uninhibited and far less hypocritical. If you could see how the whites stab each other in business and social life, you would soon know what I mean and you would agree with me.'

'I can hardly understand you,' replied Dodane. 'You speak like a highly educated man. What do you do?'

'Actually, I am a bit of a sham. I don't fully understand these words myself. I am quoting a man for whom I work, who is a very intelligent man and is deeply concerned with the black man's problems.'

'This is very interesting. I would like to meet him.'

'If you are truly interested in the good of your people, he would be very pleased to meet you as well. When can you come to a gathering?'

'This weekend I am not on shift.'

'Meet me on Saturday afternoon at four o'clock at the Orlando bus terminal. My name is Max Mtengu.'

'I am Dodane Qolotoke.'

The meeting was held in a house in a remote and ill-lit street in the new Soweto. Those attending the gathering approached the meeting place carefully, making sure that they were not observed, particularly by police or any of the known informers. The system of informers established and exploited by the South African police was probably the best in the world – it had to be to make such small resources effective against the daily growing numerical superiority of the blacks, who were always identified as the criminal element in society.

When Max Mtengu and Dodane arrived the main room of the house was already nearly full and they squeezed into a corner of the room. Looking around him, Dodane saw that the vast majority were men, but of all ages. In the welter of voices he picked out Zulu, Xhosa and Sotho in the main. The standard of dress was good and many of the men had briefcases on the floor next to them. Dodane felt his pulse quicken with excitement and impatience. Eventually a curtain on the far side of the room was parted and a tall, distinguished looking black man stepped into the room. There was a hush as he remained standing and faced the assembly in silence for a few moments. Then he raised his right arm, the hand curled into a fist, and said in a deep and powerful voice, 'Freedom.'

'Freedom!' they all responded and then the man began to speak. In the next hour Dodane learnt more of the history and circumstances of the black man than he had found out in his entire life. The answers to his questions were beginning.

But as the talk continued Dodane began to realise that this very intelligent man of Max's was not answering Dodane's main worry of why black and white had to be considered irreconcilable: why must they be different; why could they not share?

Dodane had heard of apartheid and understood that it represented the opposite of what he saw as justice for all citizens. This very intelligent man seemed to be defending the concept as he began to speak of homelands and removals of people from areas where they had lived all their lives. He was trying to make it sound like great concessions on the part of the white government.

The speaker was winding up his talk and finished with a triumphant '... we will be freed of bondage and our homelands returned to us for us to do as we will.'

Dodane could wait no longer and jumped to his feet. 'For us to starve and to be buried in the barren lands of our forefathers?'

Standing at the back of the room was a tall middle-aged man. He was dressed in a neat brown suit. He wore horn-rimmed spectacles and a briefcase lay on the floor at his feet. He looked sharply at Dodane when he spoke up.

The very intelligent man had reacted to Dodane's question with a look of distaste.

'Nonsense,' he replied. 'Our cattle will again cover the hillsides and our crops the valleys. With the help and finance of the white man, our own doctors and lawyers and priests will administer us and our businesses will be conducted by our own kind for our own benefit. White and black will be neighbours but we will be independent and will rule ourselves.'

The man at the back of the room stepped forward and adjusted his spectacles. There was a silence as he looked at Dodane.

'Have you nothing to say to this, young man?' he asked Dodane.

'I have many thoughts, but not the words,' he replied.

'Then perhaps you may agree with what I have to say.' He turned to the very intelligent man and continued. 'You know as well as I do that the whites will never let us alone to live in our ways, and I think this is just as well.'

'Firstly, there are far too many of us to be supported by the land which you have indicated is to be allotted to us. Secondly, the modern black man would never submit to the type of rule which would be imposed by many of the new chiefs. We all know that the black man in power can so often be a tyrant, a sadist and a self-seeker. Now, with the added evil tricks of the white man up his sleeve as well, he would use absolute power to crucify his people.'

'Your words indicate that you have thought deeply about this matter. Whether or not you are right is another question,' replied the very intelligent man. 'But do you have any alternative proposals?'

'Yes. Simply said, we must share this land with the whites. We must have equal rights over property, position and voice in public affairs. As the majority, we must have the greater say in the rule. But we need the white man. We need his knowledge, his wealth, his industrial capability, his voice overseas. We have the numbers, the labour, but this must be for the good of all and more particularly at this stage for those of us who have the desire and the ability to rise above the position of mere labourers.'

Dodane was entranced. Here was the synthesis and expression of his own confused thinking. Here was the truth that had eluded him ever since he had learned to think. Here was the bridge over the gulf between black and white. He was annoyed and frustrated at his lack of knowledge and his ignorance of words such as this great man had uttered.

The house in which they sat was a shabby little wood and iron shack surrounded by many more shanties just like it. The dusty street outside was a playground for the children, rubbish disposal for most and sewerage for many. Hens scratched in the dirt and lean dogs ferreted in the litter. Brightly dressed pimps and painted whores mingled with the half-naked, pot-bellied children.

Strangely, over all, above the noise of quarrels and dog fights, above the smells and the shouts, rising above the cacophony of congestion, there was laughter: the laughter of Africa that laughs because it finds something amusing in almost everything, even sometimes, in death itself.

The very intelligent man was speaking. 'Your ideas are very interesting, but of course impractical and idealistic. How could your vision ever become a reality? We have neither the resources nor the ability to create such a state.'

'I am speaking of revolution,' the tall man said grimly. 'We must overthrow the present system before we can create our own.'

'But, with no vote what can we do?' protested the other.

'Violence. The way of all history. Terrorise all who oppose us until they become as meek as we wish before we manipulate them to suit ourselves.'

'But, still, we do not have the means. The state is strong, the police efficient, the white man is not a fool, nor do we have any real leaders.'

The tall man took a deep breath and squared his shoulders. 'There are powers of which you have never heard, who wish to assist us. There are countries beyond our borders, whose thirst for justice for us is as intense as our own.

'I am able to tell you of great plans being made for us, in which we will all have a part to play; but leaders are needed. We must supply our own men to be trained to become leaders and trusted members of all our communities, to spread the news and bind the people together in common cause.

'It is men such as you,' he pointed at Dodane, 'who must lead our people, but who must first be trained for a difficult task.'

Dodane would have agreed to any suggestion coming from this golden tongue. He felt that here was his chance for knowledge, education and the power that these always bring.

He never returned to the mine.

Chapter 6

The death-like spirit of night sleep had gone back to his resting place in the cool of the thatch. The more lively day sleep spirit was on the old man's shoulder ready to seal his fluttering eyelids in the warmth of the sun.

First, Fakuwe would have whatever breakfast Ntsembu had prepared for him and then, perhaps, a short walk down to the river before settling down for the morning's dreams.

He slowly lowered himself to a squatting position next to the fire and his old wife handed him a dish of coarse mielie meal porridge which he ate in silence, then handed back the dish.

'There is a difference today,' he said.

'The food is strange?' Ntsembu asked.

'No, not in the food. Something has changed. The day brings something new. I feel it.'

'Now you dream with open eyes, old man.'

'No, woman, there is a gladness and a sorrow in the heart. I must sleep. Perhaps the dreams will make this feeling take a body.'

Ntsembu shook her head sadly and, picking up her hoe, went slowly down the path to the river. Fakuwe slumped against the wall of the hut and closed his eyes.

As always, Dodane was his dream. The stories of the letter became well loved or feared goblins weaving their way through his slumbering mind. Sometimes Dodane was but a vague image, blurred and unsmiling. This morning, as he had expected, it was different. He stirred restlessly in his sleep as the vision of his son became clear – here was Dodane the man, the youth of yesteryear – and, wonder of wonders, he heard him speak.

'My father sleeps like a carefree child.'

He felt a hand on his shoulder and then he realised that he was no longer dreaming. This was his son; Thixo had sent Dodane back to him at last. He now stood before him, tall, strong, smiling.

The old man struggled to his feet and grabbed his son by the shoulders. Dodane saw tears of joy in his father's eyes and felt his own become moist. Then he laughed and, lowering the old man to the ground again, he squatted in front of him.

'Dodane, my son. You have returned to your father and your people,' Fakuwe said breathlessly. 'Thixo is good. And my son is well?'

'My father's son is well, yes.'

'You have finished with the mines, the gold, the city?'

'I have done with the mines. I have finished working for the white man.'

'You have returned with much wealth and paper money to live the life of our fathers?'

'No. That life will never be again. This much have I learnt: that the days of the tribe are over. The black races must move on to a new way of life. Soon we will all live like the whites do.'

Fakuwe was puzzled. He had never been further than the sea, three miles from his kraal. His widely travelled son was speaking strangely.

'But you will not return to work for the white man?'

'No.'

'How and where will you live? And have you come back to us after all these days just to tell us that you are leaving again?'

'I will live in the cities. I leave tomorrow for Durban. But I will see to it that you are well provided for. And perhaps I will be able to see you again.'

Fakuwe now understood why his intuitive gladness had been tempered by sadness.

'You went to the mines for five years, my son. What has been your life? The money you have sent has barely kept us alive.

And if you are to live in the cities and not return to the mines, what work will you do? You say you will no longer work for the white man, but we must work to live and who else has the power to give us work to do? And if you go only to Durban, why can you not say that you will return often to see us?'

'My father has nothing but questions, but I will answer all. I have many things to say, to tell you, but these things must be between us only. No word must pass your lips. You must not even say that you have seen me. I intend to work against the white man for a share of what is equally our land.'

'I have a certainty that what my son has to tell me I shall have to discuss with Thixo, but, other than that I will be silent.'

Dodane began to speak and when he had finished, old Fakuwe shook his grizzled head slowly from side to side.

'Hayi, my son, your words trouble me. I understand very little of what you say, but I feel something telling me that you are very wrong.'

'Wrong? To desire and to work for the good of our people? How can it be wrong to yearn for the return of our peoples' rights in the land of our forefathers?'

'The desire can not be wrong. I long to see my lands again covered by cattle and crops, which is now impossible. For me to want to remove from Mgulu the property he has rightfully won by his industry would be equally wrong. Your desire is good, yes, but what you would do is wrong.

'Yes, the past is dead. The Xhosa and the Zulu are scattered. You have said yourself that the way of the tribe is no longer. What will you restore by trying to wrest from the white man the fruit of his labour, his victories, his greater power?'

'The dignity of our race and the repossession of our land.'

'Neither of which would feed me.'

'We do not aim to drive out the white man. Those over the seas who have our good at heart, have explained how much we do need the white man. But we must have the control of the land, we must be free in our own country, we must have authority and the position of power that is surely justified by our greater numbers.'

'A hundred jackals, my son,' the old man said sadly, 'are not the equal of one lion.' Then he continued. 'These teachers of yours over the seas, what gain is theirs?'

'Only the knowledge that justice has been done.'

In silence Fakuwe looked long and hard at his son. His steady gaze and the unmistakeable question of his expression momentarily unnerved Dodane.

'My son, for all his travelling, learning and wealth, is still but a child,' he said quietly, almost to himself.

Angry with himself and his father, Dodane stood up.

'And my father is so old he can see no further than the edge of his barren mielie field.'

'You are right, my son, but I can see the mountains in the distance.' He lifted a wrinkled arm and waved at the purple ridge that shimmered far to the north. 'I know that they have watched over my people and their lands since the sun began and they always will.

'I know that when my mielie field is a wasted patch of lifeless soil for ever and when my son is buried in the ashes of his own fire, and when the spirit of Fakuwe sits silently in the thatch, the mountains will still watch, unmoved for all man's foolishness.'

'My father has lived in the place of the doves for so long that he fears the cutting down of the trees.'

'The place of the doves is the harvest of the snake, my son. The sound of the doves nesting is always the moment for *inyushu* to strike.'

Chapter 7

Fakuwe came slowly up the steps to the verandah of the shop. A few old men, such as himself, were sitting in the shade, smoking and quietly discussing the important matter of cows, goats, sheep, crops and millet beer. Occasionally one of them would remove his pipe from his mouth and spit a long thin stream of dark spittle and tobacco juice through his blackened teeth.

The greetings were grunted and Fakuwe entered the shop, gathering his faded blanket around him. He shuffled up to the counter near the office and, purely by chance of course, near the big tilting drawer of tobacco.

Van Deventer emerged from the office and greeted the old man.

'*Molo,* Fakuwe, *usaphila.* How are you?' Then he reached into the drawer, just as Fakuwe knew he would, and placed a fistful of coarse leaves on the counter in front of Fakuwe. He acknowledged the gift with a nod. Then he said, '*Goed, dankie,*' the only two words of Afrikaans he knew, and cackled with mirth at the strange sounds his mouth had made.

'There is a short note from Dodane,' said Van Deventer. 'He says he has a very good job making English into Xhosa for the white men and English into Xhosa for the black people.'

'And this is work?' Fakuwe was astounded.

'Of course. Work is not always done with the hands. Dodane is now clever enough to work with his head.'

'But on the mines was not work with the hands?'

'Yes, but the boy has come far since then. He is now a man and is what is called educated, schooled. His brain is now stronger than his arms.'

'*Inkosi,* I can speak only to you of this. It will not pass you, I know, but Dodane is strange. He wishes me not to speak of this, but you are our friend. He was here to tell me many things. He says he will no longer work for the white man, but you tell me that he is working for the white man, even if only with his head.'

'Perhaps, old man, he feels that he is not working for the white man, but for his own people. These white people he is working among are healers of the sick and in helping them to understand the black people Dodane is assisting these people of Thixo to heal his people.'

'*Ewe,* this sounds right. But still he has strange ideas which I do not think the white man would like.'

'For all his learning, Fakuwe, Dodane is still young and all young men have times in their lives like this. Can you not remember back to your youth? Surely you had differences with the headman or even with the chief?'

'No, *Inkosi*, my youth has fled from my head just as surely as it has deserted my limbs and my loins. I can remember nothing beyond the day my son left for the mines of iGoli and the life of the white man, and even this memory is clouded and uneasy in my dreams, because it is a stranger that returned, not my son.'

'Nonsense, old one. Of course it is your son. But he has aged, as we all have. He has changed, yes, as have we, but he still knows and loves and cares for his old father.' Van Deventer took a five pound note out of the till. 'Look, he has sent this from his first wages, and says in his letter that his father must have a fine new blanket for the winter. And more money will come for your needs as he earns it.'

The old black looked longingly at the money and involuntarily pinched the thin cloth of his faded blanket. He looked up at Van Deventer and stared at him steadily until the trader shifted his gaze and, with a sharp gesture, pushed the money across the counter. Fakuwe shook his head.

'No, *Inkosi* Van,' he said sadly, 'my son has sent no money. It is your good heart that would try to replace the heart of a father's son. But, no matter how big your heart, it can not. When the father's heart is old and beats feebly, it is only the strength of the son's heart that can sustain it.'

He turned away and, leaving the tobacco and the money on the counter, he shambled out of the shop and down the steps. He went to sit in the shade of a large eucalyptus tree and allowed the tears to run unchecked down his weathered cheeks until they made droplets of mud in the soil between his feet.

Van Deventer stood in the doorway of the shop and stared at him for a long time. Conflicting emotions of anger, frustration and pity churned within him. He turned away, thinking that a brandy was necessary and hurried back to his office, kicking a startled mongrel that slept in the patch of sun near the door.

'Why do we live, Mgulu. What is living?' Fakuwe blew out a plume of smoke as he asked his question.

Mgulu patted his bulging stomach. 'Some will say that we live to eat. Others say that we exist to loosen our tightness into women. Others that we live because this is the wish and the glory of Thixo. But to me it is all a mystery. We live, it would seem, to no purpose. Death claims us all whether we have been rich or poor, sickly or well. It is not concerned with how many wives we have had, nor can our herds and crops stand between us and the earth into which we must one day sink.'

'Then has Thixo no use for us after our life? Does our spirit haunt the caves and valleys of the Amatolas, for ever lost. Is there no difference between the spirit of the good man and that of the evil man?'

'This only Thixo can answer, my friend. Perhaps the answer is in death itself.'

'Then surely I will soon know.'

'My friend's spirit feels the call of the distant hills?'

'My spirit had but one hope: my son. But, although he has returned, he is lost and divided from his people by more than the hills and rivers and valleys of the land.'

'You have seen Dodane. He is back?'

'*Ewe.* But a strange spirit lives within him. He is lost.' Fakuwe went on to tell Mgulu of his son's visit and his puzzling new way of life.

'But why does the boy think he must lead the blacks against the whites? Are the wars not long over?'

'He thinks that we are the dogs of the white man.'

'What foolishness is this? If he thinks this, then where does the dog have the right to turn on its master? My dog is well fed and has all he needs. If he bites me he is mad!'

'Dodane says our people in the cities do not have everything. They have very little of what he calls freedom. They labour endlessly with no visible end to their toil.'

'So do the ants of the kraal. See how they hurry and work all day for food alone. And having nothing can mean everything, and everything can mean nothing.'

'How do you say this, my friend?'

Mgulu took his pipe from his mouth and with the stem scratched his head, knocking his nightcap askew. 'Here, on the lands of our fathers, we have everything of one life and nothing of the other – the white man's life – either good or bad. In the city, they have everything of the white man, in their own measure, but nothing of the tribe, our freedom, our life that does not alter from day to day. Who can have everything?'

Chapter 8

Dodane pushed his way through the crowded market. The smells of spices and curries and teeming, sweating humanity lay heavily in the humidity. The Durban summer sun beating down on the iron roof of the market as intensely as it drew water vapour out of the sea and into the air, turned the inside of the building into a vast steam oven.

White shoppers drooped around, bravely defying the searing heat in their quest for what they considered to be a bargain. The merchants, ignoring or possibly not even noticing the heat, sang out the litany of their wares and watched, hawk like, for any sign of interest on the face of an unsuspecting window-shopper.

Any tourist, always immediately recognisable, would be pounced on, harried and propositioned by each stallholder in turn, as he struggled through the throng. The air, already overburdened, was laden with the yells, pleas, cries and even tears of negotiation. A sale concluded on the original asking price left the merchant strangely depressed, cheated out of the real enjoyment of doing business – to haggle!

Dodane, eyes and ears trained to observe and record everything, saw pornography viciously peddled to schoolboys. He overheard hurried arrangements made between white men and certain merchants who sold the inexhaustible commodity (which did not exclude the services of their sisters) even more fervently, it seemed, than they did their goods on display.

Money, the grease of greed, changed hands continually as feverish fingers, acquiring assumed bargains, forced it into the hands of the dusky profiteers. Pickpockets did a roaring trade.

Dodane noticed with pleasure that the young Indian women in their colourful saris around lissome and provocative bodies, were very beautiful. A warmth uncoiled itself in his loins. No matter what the others said, a man could not be expected to work effectively without the release of this natural energy which had but one outlet. He decided that he would have an Indian woman whenever he wanted.

He intended to start the reign of terror he had planned by inciting the blacks against the Indians. The Indian exploitation of the Zulus was a well-known fact and the hatred so generated should be easy to convert into energy and action. He was primed with names and places and a pocketful of money, probably the most essential ingredient of all. He also knew that, as a Xhosa, he would not have an easy task.

Outside the market building, where the heat curdled the tarmac on the edges of the road where it met the concrete of the gutter, Dodane headed for the bus terminal where there were always crowds and the prospect of gleaning information. He wandered around until he spotted an intelligent looking *umfaan* of about twelve years old.

'Where do I find him?' he asked without preamble.

'Who?'

'Tutulla.'

The boy stood silent, expressionless, but Dodane was not deceived for a second. He took out a note and repeated his question. The boy took the money. 'Come,' he said tersely.

A few blocks away from the bus terminal they entered an eating house and the *umfaan* pointed at a large Zulu standing behind the dirty counter. The lad then disappeared.

'You want something?' asked the Zulu.

'Tutulla.'

'Why ask me?' The man's eyes had widened for a second and he quickly composed himself, but not before Dodane had realised that he was on the right track.

'Do not waste my time,' Dodane growled. 'I am not playing games.'

'Why would anyone want Tutulla, that is if one knew how to contact him?' asked the other.

'It is my own business and of great importance to him and to all of us. Now stop your pretence. How do I see Tutulla?'

'But you must know that one cannot simply go and see Tutulla. These things have to be arranged.'

'Then arrange it,' Dodane demanded.

As the Zulu hesitated, Dodane took a wad of notes out of his pocket and threw it on to the counter. 'Take what you want for yourself and give the rest to the next contact but be sure to get word to Tutulla that Dodane wants to talk with him without delay. I will return tomorrow.'

It took three days and another wad of money before Dodane received permission and directions to visit the great one.

Tutulla, better known as Mr Jerome Seseni, B.A. Llb., was a tall, thin, bespectacled man. Quietly spoken, gracious and retiringly intellectual, he was a brilliant lawyer. He was able to obtain the acquittal or conviction of a client at will it seemed and the result was always determined by the financial standing of the accused or his relationship to Tutulla's cause – or both.

Seseni was the centre of a vast network of organised crime and vice which provided him with a cash, tax free income that would have supported thousands of his own people and which was culled almost exclusively from them.

He controlled the growing and distribution of dagga, the hashish of

South Africa, and spent huge sums in establishing new fields as the police waged their relentless war against the evil leaf. He was master to myriad pimps and whores and the country's largest car theft operation took its directives from him. Burglars who failed to pay tithes to the Seseni administration found themselves the subject of an informer's visit to the police.

Every penny he spent was expected to give him back a hundredfold, but never did he see to the defence or pay the fines of any of his employees or messengers who fell into the hands of the vigilant police – the risks of disclosure were too great. He was respected, even in white society, and was at pains not to invite suspicion to cast its shadow on the road to riches.

'Good morning, Mr Qolotoke,' he said, extending a well-manicured hand. 'I do not think I have had the pleasure of meeting you before?'

'No, we have not met before.'

'You are from these parts? Natal, perhaps?'

'No, but that is immaterial.' Dodane waved his hand dismissively. The lawyer smiled.

'I see; however, my informants tell me that you have been very insistent that you meet me on a matter of very great importance. As you have spent large sums of money on this, I must at least assume that the matter is of much importance. Please sit down.' He gestured towards a chair before the desk and then sat down himself.

'I am approaching you for help,' said Dodane and was amused at the veil which drew over the lawyer's eyes and the hardening of the previously urbane expression. 'Not for myself,' he continued, 'but for our people, yours and mine, the black people. Not that I expect you to lose financially, of course.' He noticed that the veil began to lift. 'I am quite prepared to pay any fee you may require and any expenses incurred. In addition, the by-products of the help you may wish to give me will certainly yield a rich harvest.'

He saw the greed in the cruel, dark eyes as the lawyer replied. 'Of course your words interest me, Mr Qolotoke, but as a lawyer I require some brief. I am still unaware of what sort of assistance you require.'

'I do not speak to you as a lawyer, Tutulla.'

Seseni's face hardened again. He pressed a button on the desk and immediately the door opened and two men came into the room.

'Look carefully at this man, Seseni said. 'Imprint his face on your memory. When he leaves here, or rather, if he leaves here, you will follow him everywhere and never let him out of your sight. Now go.'

When they had closed the door behind them, the lawyer turned to his visitor. 'Mr Qolotoke, please understand this well. From now on you are in very grave danger. Should you fail to convince me that you are entirely above suspicion, you will never leave this building alive. As you heard, you will be followed at all times with death on your shoulder. You have been indeed privileged to penetrate this deep into Tutulla's world but must now pay the price. Now proceed.'

Dodane sat back and regarded the lawyer steadily for half a minute then he spoke. 'Admitting firstly that everyone's prime interest is usually in one's own good, what else, Tutulla, is your greatest desire? With your wealth and power and social acceptability, the usual wants of a man are easily satisfied.

'Is there nothing, however, perhaps seemingly even out of the reach of your great resources and ability, that attracts you, fascinates you?'

'At the risk of seeming complacent, I must say no. But it is evident that you think there is something with which I should be concerned.'

'What about your people?'

'Am I a king, a ruler, a president? And if so, who are my people, and what of them?'

'The people I refer to are our race, the black people, no matter what tribal allegiance each may have. You have no direct power or recognised channel of authority over anyone, but it is educated people like yourself, black or white, who should have an equal voice in the affairs of our land. People like you should openly direct and govern the affairs of all citizens.'

'You know I have no vote. A white railway ganger who has failed standard four at school has a voice. I am dumb.'

'That is what must change, or be changed. This is why I and numerous colleagues are here and everywhere in the country.'

'Are you advocating subversion, revolution, communism or just a new political party?'

'All of these. At the moment subversion and sabotage and terror. Later the welding together of our people into a great communal citizenship. But first we must show our strength and our organisational capacity. We must hit organised society, the establishment, where it hurts most: in its pocket, its pride and its supposed strength. We will instigate strike after strike against the white man and his rule. Then, when he totters and falls, we lift him up, we absorb him. We need him but as part of us, not lord of us.'

'You are a starry-eyed idealist.'

'With plenty of practical knowledge, however.'

'And where do I come into all this? What is my role and where is my benefit, other than, of course, the liberation of my people?'

Dodane would have liked to put his fist squarely in the mocking, cruel mouth as it framed the sarcastic words, but he merely said, 'You provide the resources.'

'Be specific.'

'To begin with I would want to strike a note of terror. I would like to conduct something that would start people thinking along the right lines, that is, that we are a force to be reckoned with.

'I am sure that something positive could be made of the bad feeling that seems to exist between the Indians and the Zulus. Granted the Indians are not whites, but they are a menace to everyone and their elimination will serve a double purpose: we get rid of them, take them off the back of our people, and we terrorise the whole city, having people wondering whom and where we will strike next. I am sure the whites would get the message.

'What I need is the help of your organisation in making a move against the Indians completely effective. I need a full scale riot, plenty of bloodshed and burnings and the destruction of every Indian business and as many homes as possible.

'You have the men. I have the training and the ability to organise them in such a project. If you want me to pay them, I will and, in addition, all the loot of the shops will be yours to dispose of at your will.'

Seseni arose and went to a cabinet against the wall behind the desk. He extracted a bottle of Chivas Regal and two Waterford glasses. He poured two heavy measures of neat spirit and handed one to Dodane.

'To the liberation of our people!'

Dodane downed his drink in a single gulp. He had not expected such a rapid and easy convincing of Tutulla. 'I take it then, that you are prepared to help me?'

Seseni thought that in all probability he would only be helping himself, but he replied, 'No, not you. I will help my people through you. But remember, I still know nothing of you. But I have no time to spend in checking up on you. However, as you heard my instructions, you will be watched at all times during your preparations and I shall need to be completely satisfied of your integrity. If there is any suggestion of your contacting any undesirable third parties you will be eliminated without warning or fuss.'

'Good enough,' replied Dodane. 'Now for the details.'

The lawyer interrupted him. 'No, I do not want to know anything of your plans. You must do what you will; have no fear, I will be informed. Besides your two bodyguards,' he smiled evilly, 'I will assign someone trustworthy to assist you.'

He brought out the bottle once more and poured. Then he sat back and said genially: 'Now I happen to have some spare time. We can look deeply into this very excellent bottle while you tell me all there is to know about yourself. Omit nothing. That would be very wise.'

Dodane was pleased to see the large number of men assembled in the meeting place. He had profound assurances from Tutulla's man who had organised the gathering that every delegate was 'clean' and not an informer. It had taken a week to make the arrangements and now many black men, mostly well dressed and carrying briefcases, were waiting in a buzz of excitement for the unknown Dodane to address them.

'Friends,' he said, speaking slowly and in a deep voice which carried to the back of the hall, 'I hope that in years to come we will all be able to look back on this night as the turning point in the black man's struggle to gain his freedom. Tonight I wish to describe to you the plight of our brothers all over this land which should be ours, and my ideas of how we can begin the revolution against the system which enslaves us.

'When I have convinced you of my integrity and the wisdom of our plans I will ask for your assistance in taking this message with you throughout the city to prepare our people for a simultaneous rising that will strike fear into all who despise us or who might resist us.'

He was interrupted by a thickset, coal black Zulu who stood up and demanded, 'Who are you, a Xhosa, to dare even to speak thus to the Zulu? Who are you to call us to yourself like so many Fingoes to do your bidding?'

Dodane controlled his temper: 'I am no one, that is true, but I am the bearer of good news of much assistance for our cause as black men in slavery. Xhosa or whatever is unimportant, I am the one who is trained in the ways necessary to bring the white man to his knees.'

'Never,' shouted the Zulu, 'never is there such a Xhosa. You are but stray dogs. I will not heed you!'

Dodane sighed and realised that the time had come to assert himself. Another element of his training would be put to the test. He stepped away from the rostrum and walked slowly down to where the man stood quivering with anger. He smiled at him.

'You will not co-operate?'

The Zulu spat in Dodane's face.

Dodane's right hand, the edge of his palm rock hard, flashed forward and pulped the man's larynx. His knee jerked upwards crushing the man's testicles into his perineum. As the man folded, Dodane caught his left arm and twisted it savagely, holding the Zulu's body on the floor with his foot as he wrenched the arm upwards until the elbow and shoulder were totally dislocated.

Leaving the senseless man on the floor, he returned to his place at the top of the room and quietly continued his discourse. 'This is not the time or place to let childish matters such as origins occupy our thoughts and energies.' He looked with amusement at the stunned faces of his listeners. His controlled but effective violence had shocked even their toughened sensibilities. The man on the floor lay motionless.

'As a Xhosa, I will ignore any claims to superiority that you Zulus or anyone wish to make. I am not interested in myself, in my future, my position, nor for that matter, my tribe. Nor am I interested in any of you individually, in any way. I am here only to serve the cause of freedom in this country and I want you to do the same. The future of the black man is greater, even than the pride of the Zulu,' he concluded with a slight smile.

A spokesman got to his feet and said: 'Very well, we will hear you out. Please continue.'

'Good. Our first move will be against the Indians. We will demonstrate our strength and the extent of our ability to be organised by striking every Indian shop and home and business at the same time with a view to eliminating them from this city. Now I want to hear from each of you in turn just what you do, how you are connected, where you can best organise men and communicate with them and what you know of the city.'

The discussion continued into the early hours of the morning when, after setting the time of their next meeting, Dodane closed the proceedings and prepared to leave. The Zulu was still on the floor where he had fallen. Someone examined him and said, 'He's dead.'

'Well then, dispose of it,' said Dodane, and walked out into the first glow of dawn.

The rising was planned for the 14th September. By the 12th of the month many sectors of the city were picketed by loafing blacks, a fact which did not go unnoticed by the police, who built up their forces and watched for the first signs of trouble.

The police enjoyed probably the best network of informers in the world and they had received reports of secret meetings over the past few weeks and rumours of coming unrest. They even had a description of a Xhosa who was said to be behind the disturbance but they could not track him down, nor could they obtain any reasonable estimate of a date on which to expect trouble.

The tension in the poorer sections of the city and particularly in the Indian business district was electric but still the police could not marshall adequate facts, even from the best of their black agents.

If the uprising had exploded as planned, the consequences would have been catastrophic. Even the extremely well-informed and well-prepared police force would have been unable to quell the massacre in its devilish perfection of timing and concerted action as devised by Dodane.

However, it was on the 13th September, a day early, that an unrelated accident caused a misfire of the plan which although largely foiled, nevertheless resulted in two days of blood, fire and plunder.

A grubby little *piccanin* was playing on the pavement outside an Indian shop when he noticed a tray of tomatoes leaning against the wall next to the door of the shop. Driven by the rumblings of his seldom filled stomach, he sidled up to the tray and quickly filched a plump red fruit.

The shopkeeper saw him and rushed out, screaming at the little black urchin who took to his heels and fled out into the road directly into the path of a fast-moving car. The driver of the car, also an Indian, had no chance of avoiding him and struck him squarely, throwing his body into the gutter outside the shop. Before the lifeless body of the child had stopped quivering, a group of enraged blacks converged on the car and pulled the screaming man from his seat. They literally tore him to pieces and flung his dismembered body into the car which they set alight.

Then they turned their attention to the shopkeeper who, very soon, was a pile of charred flesh in his fiercely burning shop.

The news was carried swiftly from street to street and block to block and the waiting rioters, assuming that they had the wrong details concerning the date, began to implement instructions. Inevitably, of course, they were disorganised. Instead of the rising being simultaneous throughout the city, the groups of blacks began their rioting one by one as the news reached them. The police acted so swiftly that numerous units of the rioters did not have the chance to go into action at all.

A cursing Dodane raced around the trouble spots. Realising that it was too late to stop the action and intent on salvaging his planned operations, he spurred on the gangs.

He gathered a group of leaderless men and went from point to point, burning, looting, killing and raping. He burst into a shop where he was confronted by a frightened old man and a young woman. The old man began to plead but Dodane sent him to his death with one backhanded swipe. As the girl began to scream, he tore the clothes from her body and threw her to the floor. At first she struggled and kicked but suddenly was still. She stared up at Dodane as he forced himself into her. 'I will never forget your face,' she gasped as it contorted in a bestial orgasm.

A siren wailed outside and Dodane, failing to silence the screaming girl, fled through the shop and the house behind it and into the lanes and alleyways in search of another target.

It was when he and a number of his group were trying to set fire to a mosque that they were surprised by a police force and arrested. Dodane was overpowered, handcuffed and thrown into the back of a police van. The fire brigades steadily gained control of the fires and the police routed and rounded up many of the leaderless rioters. But hundreds of Indians had lost their lives; homes and businesses had been destroyed and the womenfolk had been repeatedly raped.

At the line-up of prisoners, there was no mistaking the Xhosa and unhesitatingly the Indian girl pointed him out as her rapist and the killer of her father.

Chapter 9

A fly had found the droplet of spittle that had bubbled between Fakuwe's lips as he slept and it buzzed around in a fever of excitement. It landed on his upper lip and rubbed its feet together in an ecstasy of anticipation. But the ticklish passage across the sleeping man's lips awakened him and he sat up with a grunt and a little snort, passing a hand across his mouth. The fly departed, losing his precious drop to the old man's hand.

Fakuwe stretched his limbs and blinked. The sun was strong and he had slept deeply. Sleep was the balm for all his sorrows: both sadness and hunger were forgotten in the sealing of the eyes.

He listened to the song of the women in the lands across the river. Their voices were high-pitched and clear. They sang to the soil that they were loosening, telling it to open wide its arms for the seed, to suckle it well and then to send it forth into the sun, strong, fresh and fruit-bearing. Fakuwe's smile was sad as he listened to their song.

He looked down the hillside to where his meagre crop browned a patch in the green of the long grass. He saw Ntsembu coming up the slope towards him. She looked old and tired as, using her hoe as a staff, she clambered wearily up the crooked path.

Far across the lands, beyond the green hills rolling away, above the heat haze that danced without tiring until the sun himself tired of the day, at the very edge of Fakuwe's world, the mountains purpled the horizon. Heavily they lay. Long had they slept. Fast-locked they held the secret of Fakuwe's world. With Fakuwe's father's father of centuries, the mountains slept. Oh mountains of the edge of the world, would that my son could sleep with you and see your silent side placed firmly on the edge of his world, these lands.

Ntsembu had come up to Fakuwe. She placed the hoe on the ground, dropped to her knees and then sat back on her haunches.

'*Molo,*' she said. Good day.

'*Ewe,*' the old man mumbled. He looked at her, half closing his eyes against the brilliance of the sun. 'I have slept well this morning,' he continued.

'Truly have you slept, old man. The sun is always your friend these days.'

'But I have dreamed,' he replied.

'We dream daily, old one; our dreams take us to but one world.'

'This is true, but each dream gives me more of this world.'

'With the return of Dodane we shall know the truth of our dreams.'

'The return may never be.'

'It will be. Thixo is good.'

Ntsembu arose and took the hoe into the hut and hung it between the thatch and the top of the mud wall. Then she began to break off *nkobes,* the hard dried mielies, into the black three-legged pot. She listened to the old man talking to her as she worked.

'Again I dreamed of our son, Dodane. I saw him in the bottom of the world as he wielded the pick of the white man for the white man's gold. Around him were others of his race and others not of his race. But they worked together. I saw Dodane fling down his pick and cry out for the sun; cry out that the sun called him.'

'Thus have you dreamed all these years, old man,' replied Ntsembu. 'But when Dodane calls out for the sun your dream shows the woman of shame, unclothed, with the breasts of gold, who leads him back to the pick and allows his caresses as a reward when the pick is taken up once more.'

'Yes, woman, thus have the years brought my dream. But today the pick lay where it had fallen and the breasts of gold I saw to be spurned and to melt.'

Ntsembu looked up from her cooking. Fakuwe was leaning back, his eyes half closed and, although he had ceased speaking, his lips still moved. He was speaking to Thixo, the God of his fathers, the Maker of Rain, Preserver of Crops and Guardian of Sons. The old woman shook her head slowly. 'Aau!' she said to herself, 'The man has grown old indeed. His dreams and his life are but one.'

On the other side of the river lay the lands of Mgulu. They stretched over many hills and Mgulu's yearly grass burnings, just before spring, were sights that brought viewers from many miles around, such was their size and beauty.

Mgulu was now well into planting season. His lands lay brown over the hills in freshly turned soil. Not a single dry stalk of last year's crop jutted into the air. His women were busy turning the soil of the last field and would soon begin to sow the little pebbles of gold and white for the next year's crop.

Fakuwe's land still pointed brown fingers into the sky. They crackled as they swayed in the breeze, rubbing their withered skins together. They clung fast to the unyielding soil that Fakuwe needed for his next year's food.

Tomorrow Ntsembu must begin to break off those dry fingers and use them in the fire. If Mgulu will allow it, some of his womenfolk might help her to lay a small patch of the ground bare to the seed. Then Fakuwe could sit and watch them and dream of that next crop, perhaps their last, seeing it tall and green and groaning under much fruit. He had dreamed thus through many years and had always opened his eyes to see a stunted crop of dull fruit and his old Ntsembu slowly and painfully hoeing the stubborn soil. Then his tears would flow once more and lull him back to sleep.

Fakuwe rose from his place against the wall and gathered his blanket around himself. It felt very thin between his fingers. He knew it would be the last blanket he would own in his life ... unless Dodane came home freed of his error and bringing money. He would surely buy a blanket for his old father.

He stepped away from his hut and ambled down the path. A lean black dog sprang up from its place in the shade and followed him. They headed for the river.

At a large flat rock on the far bank, some of Mgulu's women were washing clothes and rubbing red ochre into blankets spread on the stones. At the ford, Fakuwe, clutching his blanket around him, crossed by means of the stepping stones and, after greeting the women, passed on his way up the hill.

He admired the lands of Mgulu. Even his sorrow at the poor state of his own soil could not lessen the admiration due to these lands.

Mgulu's kraal lay around a shoulder of the hill. The walker comes upon the huts suddenly as he follows the path cut into the hillside by many years of feet. Fakuwe stopped short as the huts sprang into view. His reasons were to rest and to admire the size and beauty of his friend's kraal. He marvelled at the number of sheep and goats that browsed on the slopes and the many cows and oxen, straight-backed and fat, that stood beside the bend in the river where the willow trees made tents of cool shade for them in the heat of the day. Quietly content, they flicked the brushes of their tails at the lethargic flies.

Piccanins played around among the fowls and ducks and the squeals of an infant in one of the huts were echoed by the piglets that kept their mother on her side while they fought for the choicest teats.

Mgulu sat in the sun outside his main hut. His blanket was clean and ochred to an excellent shade of dark orange. He smoked a yellow pipe with a long stem and a high thin bowl. As a sign of his station and wealth he wore a pink woollen nightcap, complete with pompon, on his head and a double string of the trader's best blue beads around his neck. He was short and fat and good natured. He had five wives.

Fakuwe stepped down the gentle slope and carefully sat down beside his neighbour. Saying nothing, Mgulu handed him the pipe and Fakuwe took three quick puffs, held a fourth long draw in his mouth, and handed the pipe back. Still nothing was said. Fakuwe squeezed out his mouthful of smoke slowly, savouring the rich flavour of the brand that only the likes of Mgulu could afford and grunted his approval. He leaned back against the wall of the hut.

Without taking his eyes off the cattle and the river he greeted his friend. '*Molo, Mgulu.*'

'*Molo, mfondini.*' Hullo friend.

The greetings were over and there was a silence. It was too warm for much conversation and what was not said today could be said tomorrow. Even the day after that would provide time for the saying of things. However, Fakuwe eventually broke the silence.

'I see much work in your lands today. Your harvest should be great.'

'The women have worked well and the soil is good. Now it remains for Thixo to send the rain in due season.'

'He will send it. He is good and He loves Mgulu. This can be seen in Mgulu's good fortune.'

'But then, do you say Thixo does not love Fakuwe, because he does not prosper equally?'

'No. He loves Fakuwe just as well, that I believe. But even Thixo cannot produce women from nowhere to work the soil. I did not use properly the means he gave me to provide myself with many wives. And now He can neither pour back strength into these old limbs that I may work, nor into these loins that I may procure another wife, even if I had enough *lobola*. Neither can He be expected to strengthen Ntsembu. She too has lived her course. Thixo commands the sun and the wind, withholds or sends the rain and changes the seasons to His plan. But man He has created so, and cannot alter.'

'This is truly strange,' replied Mgulu. 'It would seem so much easier to change the little thing that is man, than to guide the sun across the sky and hang up the moon at night and fix the stars; to drive the invisible wind from the Amatolas to the sea and back again.'

'One day we shall understand Thixo.'

'As now our fathers do.'

All this talk had made a little more smoke and silence necessary and they lapsed into thoughtful grunts. But it was no surprise to Fakuwe when Mgulu spoke again saying, 'I will tell some of my young women to help Ntsembu tomorrow and until your crop is planted.'

'Thixo is good in you,' Fakuwe said and accepted the pipe again.

'You will see the great goodness of Thixo when your Dodane returns,' said Mgulu.

'You think that he will return?'

'*Ewe.* Yes. He is good. He cannot help being good and more so to those in need.'

'Aau!'

'Mhm.'

GLOSSARY

amantombi	young maidens
basela	free gift
ewe	yes
Geniet dit	Afrikaans for "Enjoy it"
iGoli	Johannesburg (lit. "the gold")
iMonti	East London (lit. "the (river) mouth")
impi	Battalion of warriors
inkosi	Master, Sir, boss.
inyushu	Boomslang – tree snake
jong	Afrikaans for joung fellow
knobkerries	strong fighting stick with enlarged end.
lobola	Payment in cattle etc. by bridegroom to father of bride
molo	Hullo
NRC	Native Recruiting Corporation – an agent for mine labour
piccanin	young boy of about five years old
qaba	a rural peasant Xhosa
shebeen	unlicensed house selling alcohol
swartgat	Afrikaans for (literally) "black backside"
Thixo	The Almighty
umcho-cho	to dance
umfaan	a young boy around puberty
umtshotsho boys	gang of youths who run long distances, together singing to the tune of a concertina or harmonica
usaphila	How are you?